SUMMER'S NIGHTMARE

INGRID JENNINGS

Summer's Nightmare
Ingrid Jennings

Lioness Publishing
Lionesspublishing@ymail.com

This is a work of fiction. Names, characters, businesses, places, events, locales, and incidents are either the products of the author's imagination or used in a fictitious manner. Any resemblance to actual persons, living or dead, or actual events is purely coincidental.

Print Edition
ISBN: 978-0-9856960-9-2

Printed in United States

Dedication

For Murelean, my mom who is my constant help and motivation.

Contents

THE BEGINNING

Gunshots pierced the summer night. One after another, spraying right in my direction. The shots thundered and bounced off the sun-bleached tombstone behind which I hid in St. Louis cemetery. Each shot shortened my breath and caused my heart to pound in every region of my body. The full moon's light lingered in the corners and crevices, the shooters hidden from my view, their direction unknown, but I could hear their muffled voices near me. My head was pressed against the engraved name of Marie Laveau and the dates 1794-1881.

"Sauve-moi chère reine accorde-moi le désir," I whispered, begging for a desperate wish from the deceased French New Orleans voodoo queen, hoping her spirit could hear my cries for mercy and forgiveness. Trapped in that gloomy cemetery, I found myself whispering to the deceased woman's tomb. My voice is a fragile offering to the beyond. With every word, I prayed that her spirit might hear my pleas and bestow upon me the mercy and forgiveness my heavy heart desperately sought.

As I crouched there, the pain of sorrow slammed down upon me, and warm tears welled up, teetering on the edge of release. They clung to the corners of my eyes, poised to cascade down and drown out anything in their path. Drawing in deep breaths, I delved into the depths of my soul, seeking fragments of strength, slivers of courage, or even the tiniest trace of adrenaline to let me make it through this horrific moment.

The air surrounding me was thick with the musty remnants of days past, tainted by the unmistakable odors of urine and feces—a grim testament to the countless homeless souls who sought refuge in this desolate cemetery. With trembling hands, I withdrew my husband's jackknife from my pocket, my fingertips tracing the engraved initials "CJ." It was a reminder of the love and protection he had once offered, now a solitary beacon of reassurance in a world gripped by darkness.

Charles James, the man who set fire to my soul, hatred stirs throughout my core when I think of him, but somewhere in the depths of my heart, there remains a deep ache for him. He would know what to do at this moment. Here I am, lost in a dream, scattered brain, I should just take my own life and end all this torment. Lord, have mercy on my soul!

With trepidation, I carefully unfolded the blade, its sharp edge gleaming ominously in the moonlight. My left pointer finger bore the brunt of the blade's sting as I punctured it, drawing forth a crimson offering. The ancient tomb of Marie Laveau loomed before me, its granite surface inscrutable in the dim glow of night. The three Xs I stained upon the tomb's surface with my blood glistened, creating an eerie tableau against the stone. A desperate yearning clawed at my heart, an insatiable hunger for the supernatural to manifest itself.

I pleaded to the unseen forces surrounding me, longing for magic to descend and weave a new tapestry of fate.

"Help me," I whispered, the words trembling on my lips like a fragile prayer. As if in response, tears streamed down my cheeks like relentless waterfalls, drenching the ash-covered white fabric of my t-shirt. My body lay there, ensnared by a potent blend of fear, sorrow, anger, depression, and gnawing uncertainty. Nearby, the crunch of footsteps upon fallen autumn leaves echoed, a haunting reminder of the threat chasing me. The ominous sounds of bullets drew nearer, a relentless percussion.

In that desolate moment, I harbored the grim certainty that this was my final chapter. I lay in the darkness at the foot of Marie Laveau's tomb, hoping our souls would cross.

AWAKENING

I awake to a disorienting world, and my senses slowly piece together the puzzle of my surroundings. The environment that envelops me tells a story of its own. My consciousness slowly unfolds in this cramped, plastic hospital twin bed, cocooned beneath a thin, powder-colored sheet that barely whispers its presence against my numb form. My gaze wanders to the stark reality of chalky white walls, their unforgiving neutrality casting a pallor over the room. The air bears a distinct chill, creeping beneath my skin and beckoning involuntary shivers that dance along my spine. Goosebumps erupt like miniature foothills, forming a tactile symphony up and down my trembling arms. Fatigue weighs upon my eyelids like lead, mingling with my thoughts, creating a haze of uncertainty. Wisps of sleepiness twist around my consciousness, entangling my cognitive threads. Questions spiral within the confines of my mind, casting a shadow of doubt over my disoriented state. "Where am I?" I mumble, my words a dry and brittle utterance, my lips chapped and peeling.

My eyes rove the confines of the minuscule, freezing chamber, trying to extract meaning from its confines. My fingers run a fretful race up and down my bumpy arms, a futile attempt to chase away the relentless chill. Beyond me, a petite square window allows a stream of light to invade the room, unveiling a sparse arrangement of furnishings. A white wardrobe stands against one wall, alongside a desk, a solitary chair, a modest nightstand beside my bed, and a plain white clock on the wall, but the time is unimportant. Curiously absent are the familiar trappings of most hospital rooms, such as telephones and boards laden with notes. The room appears to be a medical ward, yet it lacks the essential equipment that one would expect. Fright circles around my existence, leaving me to wonder— how had I come to be here?

Scanning my own body for clues, I search for any signs that might explain why I'm stuck in this hospital room. My head throbs with a punishing ache, but that alone doesn't seem like reason enough to be confined to a hospital bed. My bare feet make contact with the icy-cold linoleum floor, sending an electrifying chill up my spine. I race to the door of the room and turn the handle. Locked. Panic seizes my chest, squeezing the breath from my lungs. Seconds dwindle, and my thoughts churn in a chaotic whirlwind. It's as if I've been suspended in a never-ending slumber, a void of memory and understanding. I can't recall where I was before somehow ending up in this bewildering place. Total confusion and a queasy wave of nausea grip me, tearing at the pit of my stomach. Desperation and emptiness threaten to consume me until my breath finally steadies. But questions linger, tormenting my mind.

"What in the hell is happening?" I scream aloud. The name "Charles" escapes my lips in a plea for answers I feel only he can provide.

My fist strikes the door, and my mind doesn't even register the pain. I kick at the door, breaking a toenail in the process. A loud buzzer goes off, and a click comes from the knob. Briskly, I walk out, not caring that I'm dressed in only a white hospital gown. The cold air caresses my butt cheeks with each step. I walk a few doors down until I reach a small nurses' station at the corner.

"Hello, hello, can someone please help me!" "Charles!" I scream.

"Hey! What's all the commotion about?" a tall, slim woman with dark brown dreads in white scrubs asks me as I approach the desk. Her tone is a blend of curiosity and irritation. Her name tag reads Delisa. A crease of concern furrows her brow as she looks up from the desk.

"What's going on? Why am I here! Where is my husband!" These words aggressively spill out of my mouth with the speed of a locomotive.

The woman's features contort into a sour expression as if she had just bit down on a lemon. Her hazel eyes roll dismissively, and she sighs in exasperation. "Have a seat," she retorts, gesturing curtly toward a row of aging, dingy wicker chairs.

I square my shoulders, determination setting in. "I'll sit once you explain why I'm here. I need to use a phone to call my husband," I insist, my voice unwavering in the face of her shrewd demeanor.

"Can you just have a seat and calm down? I'll call the doctor," she says with a roll of her neck and the glare of a lioness.

My heavy breathing controls my voice, and it becomes shaky. I try to speak calmly:

"Please tell me where I am and why."

"Calm down; the doctor will explain everything."

Taking a deep breath, I smell the fresh smell of bleach and scented cleaners. I breathe out horrific fear of the unknowing and terror of what may be.

With hesitant steps, I turn away from the front desk and move slowly toward the row of worn wicker chairs. An unsettling mix of apprehension and curiosity simmer within me, demanding answers for the bewildering circumstances that led me to a locked room, where freedom requires a buzz of approval, and my memories remain veiled in darkness.

As I approach the chairs, my mind whirls with unnerving possibilities. Could this be some governmental experimentation center where unwitting individuals are subjected to unknown tests and trials? A shiver cascades down my spine at the thought of being a mere guinea pig in a larger, more ominous scheme. The desire for answers burns within me, compelling me to uncover the truth behind why I'm here.

Once I sit, I watch as the nurse picks up the phone, presses a button, and says, "Dr. Mocker, Summer James would like to know what is going on and why she's here." There is a short pause, and then, "Yep, she's right here in front of me."

She hangs up the phone and looks at me with a crooked phony smile.

"Dr. Mocker says you can go on to his office. It's down the hall to the left."

She points her long, slender finger in the direction.

"Look up," she says. I look toward the ceiling at a camera pointing down. "There are many eyes on you, and they can get to you in a heartbeat, so don't try to be smart!" She says all this with a sly smile.

Without hesitation, I push myself up from the desk and follow Delisa's indicated path. Every step I take through the halls seems engineered to amplify the sensation of being under an unrelenting watchful gaze. It sends shivers cascading down my spine, a chilling reminder of my entrapment. As I journey further into this labyrinth, my eyes can't help but catch sight of the ceiling-mounted cameras, their unblinking lenses recording every move. Paranoia clings to my every thought, and a heavy unease settles in my core. Passing one door, I instinctively slow my pace.

Inside one of the rooms, a frail, wiry-haired lady in a gray dress perches on the edge of a bed, her gaze transfixed upon the unyielding wall before her. A tranquil smile graces her lips, and for some reason, it tugs at my heartstrings. Thoughts of my mom sitting on the edge of her bed praying slide through my mind. In the room adjacent to it, a tall, bald-headed man wearing a vivid green sweatsuit, his lips moving ceaselessly, issues a stream of hushed words into the empty air. My curiosity surges, but no one else is in the room with him, leaving me to wonder about the nature of his dialogue. Further down the hallway, in another room, my eyes lock on another man, his wide grin resembling that of the Joker from Batman. He paces relentlessly across the floor, meticulously counting his steps and rubbing his hands together in a peculiar rhythm. The eerie atmosphere within these walls intensifies, leaving me to wonder about the stories concealed behind these doors. Other doors are closed, but I approach a medium bronze plaque that sits above a table with a plastic vase and artificial flowers.

Once closer, I read the plaque, which reads Brunswick Mental Health Institute. Mental health institute rolls across my mind like the waves in a soaring ocean.

How did I get trapped in a crazy house?

For a moment, I stand there and search for any memory of what got me here. Everything is blank. My mind feels empty, and my head pounds. Tears warm my cheeks, I look down, and my hands are shaking.

I continue to walk until I come to a 's door that's cracked open. It has a small bronze rectangular plaque with Dr. E. Mocker, Chief Psychiatrist, engraved on it. Right above the plaque is a camera, and I know someone is staring me in the face like a nosy neighbor hiding behind a curtain. I knock and then push open the door and walk into the office without waiting for an answer.

I step into the office of Dr. E. Mocker, and my eyes dance across the scene before me, drawn to the vivid details that paint a narrative of this peculiar space. Cream-colored walls adorned with meticulously hand-painted magnolia trees frame the room, their delicate blossoms bursting forth in vibrant hues, infusing an unexpected sense of life into the otherwise sterile atmosphere. A stately statue of a pelican perches at the side of the doctor's imposing antique espresso desk, a sentinel guarding the secrets within the room. Two grandiose bookcases, leaning against adjacent walls, beckon with their overflowing bounty of hardcover books. Each book whispers stories and knowledge, a silent testament to the depths of wisdom that might be unearthed within these walls. My gaze then wanders to four certificates, elegantly framed in opulent shades, adorning the wall behind the Victorian desk.

One bears the prestigious emblem of Louisiana State University, its golden lettering gleaming at the top. Two others proudly proclaim affiliation with the University of Miami, their ornate frames standing as a testament to academic prowess. The last certificate documents a residency at Jackson Mental Health Clinic, a reminder of the path that had led Dr. E. Mocker to this room.

I can't help but ponder the nature of pompous individuals who revel in showcasing their achievements. Engrossed in the papers within a manila folder, Dr. Mocker abruptly closes it, drawing my attention to his presence. He looks up at me and with an inviting nod, gestures to a cushioned, rich, espresso-colored chair.

"Have a seat," he beckons, his words delivered with the kind of practiced professionalism that bespeaks a man well-versed in the art of understanding the human mind. With a sense of anticipation, I sink into the plush embrace of the chair, poised for what lies ahead.

"I take it you're Dr. Mocker."

"I am."

"Can you please tell me why I am here?"

I pause for ten seconds. "Why am I here? Did something happen to me?"

All the questions spill out of my mouth like water from an overturned pitcher. My gaze lingers on the doctor, taking in the intricate details of his appearance. Although seated, his presence conveys a sense of towering height, his frame easily stretching beyond the six-foot mark. He wears a tan colored shirt beneath a brown vest. This combination harmonizes beautifully with his warm, caramel-colored skin. Handsome would be an understatement; he possesses a magnetic allure with his long brown dreads, adding a touch of mystery to his demeanor. My intuition tells me he can't be more than a youthful 30 to 40, an unusual age for one holding the esteemed title of chief psychiatrist. A small, modest gold wedding band sits on his finger, and a simple chronograph watch is on his wrist. I narrow my vision to take a closer look at his watch, a Britleying. I remember seeing one in a jewelry store in Houston's Galleria Mall. I once thought it would be an excellent gift for my husband until I saw the price tag of over $9,000. I remember thinking, How can a watch so simple cost so much? This doctor is obviously modest but has expensive taste, I guess. I see him looking over his gold-rimmed Gucci glasses as if thinking of the best way to answer my questions.

"What is the last thing you remember?" he asks me.

I search my mind for anything, and finally, I see tombstones.

Tombstones? Why do I see tombstones?

"Wait a second, I remember being at a cemetery."

"What about before you were there," he asks with a curious look on his oval-shaped face.

"I can't remember."

"Do you remember leaving the cemetery?"

"No, I was at the cemetery, then I woke up here."

"What were you doing at the cemetery."

Why would I be at a cemetery? Did someone die? Marie! I was at her grave!

"I remember being at Marie Laveau's grave and praying to her."

"What were you praying to her about?"

"I don't remember."

"Is she one of your relatives?"

"You're obviously not from New Orleans. She's the most powerful voodoo queen that ever lived in these parts. Legend says that if you go to her tomb and put three Xs on it, she will grant you a wish."

"Is that what you were doing?"

"I don't remember."

"Do you practice voodoo?"

I become very suspicious of all his questions.

"Dr. Mocker, I'm answering all of your questions, and you never answered any of mine.

"Why am I here!"

My words rise to soprano as I throw them at the doctor. "What the hell is going on?" I demand.

"Summer, yesterday afternoon, you received ECT for the second time this month. Sometimes, it can cause temporary memory loss."

"What is ECT?"

"It's short for electroconvulsive therapy. It's a treatment we use to help patients get better. While you were awaiting trial, you attempted to commit suicide on two separate occasions. This is critical. You were diagnosed as a manic depressive and bipolar, and the judge sentenced you to come here instead of jail. She also ordered that you receive ECT until you can function normally. You've been doing so well. We've made so much progress."

"What? Trial? Jail? What? I don't understand why I'm here. And what is this electrocon whatever therapy? Why would I lose my memory? Please let me call my husband."

I need to talk to Charles. This is insane! None of this makes any sense!

"Summer, I'm sorry, but I can't do that."

"Why not?" I shout.

"You can't call your husband."

"Why?"

"Calm down, and I'll explain whatever you need me to."

"There are spots in my memory like someone pulled out sections of my life."

Warm tears roll down my cheeks and land on my arms, knocking off the chill.

"It's completely normal. That can be an adverse reaction to ECT. You'll get your memory back. Sometimes, it takes a few days, but it can also be a few months, but it'll come back. Just remain calm, and I'll fill in any gaps regarding your stay here."

"My stay here? You say that like it's a vacation. What was I awaiting trial for?"

"First, I want you to calm down. Your legs are twitching, and you're rocking back and forth. Everyone at this facility is here to help you. We've helped many people. When you leave here, you'll be much better able to cope with things and the changes in your life."

"A few days or a few months? Which one, Dr. Mocker. And what was I awaiting trial for!"

Dr. Mocker looks at the stack of files on his desk. He opens a folder, closes it, and then takes a sip of coffee. He then brings his hands together, crosses his fingers, and rests them under his chin.

"Would you like a drink of water," he asks me.

"I would really like to know what I was awaiting trial for?"

"Third-degree murder," he spits out.

"Murder?"

"Yes, murder."

"I'm not a murderer. I would never murder anyone. That's impossible!"

I stand up from my chair and begin walking toward the bookcase. Quickly, I turn and walk back. Blood flushes through my body, sweat pierces my skin, and my palms heat up. My legs and feet just want to walk. Back then forth. Back then forth. My hands slide across the back of the chair. Murder playing in my mind. The song just can't stop.

"Please, Summer, have a seat," the doctor urges me.

My chest rises until it's almost level with my chin, and for a fleeting moment, I lose the rhythm of my own breath. Then, with a slow, deliberate inhalation, I regain my composure and mutter, "I'm struggling to comprehend all of this. It's just so new to me."

A few more tears wet my cheeks.

"It's not new to you, you just don't remember, but I promise it'll come back to you."

"Did I lose my memory after the other treatments?"

"Once before, but your memory returned after a few hours."

"Who was I accused of killing?"

"Have a sit and try to calm down."

I can feel ants running up and down my legs, but none were there. Heat glides against my skin. It's taking all my might to relax and sit back down in the chair. My butt hits the cushion, my mind hits the highway soaring for reality because this must be a dream.

"Who did I murder?" This time, I whisper the question. My frightened voice barely rises over the noise from the air conditioner.

I can see Dr. Mocker taking a deep breath, his Adam's apple rising up and down. He strengthens his glasses, breathes in another deep breath, and then breathes out, "You were charged with the murder of your husband. They called it a crime of passion. Your lawyer pled temporary insanity, and you were found not guilty, but because you attempted suicide, the judge deemed you a risk to yourself and others and sentenced you here for treatment and evaluation."

The words roll off this man's lips, piercing my heart in all four chambers. I gasp, my blood boiling with rage and my hands, arms, and legs trembling with anger. I can hear myself yelling, "Impossible, impossible," while getting out of my seat and stepping in a backward motion. Two people in scrubs race into the room, one man and one woman. The man is tall with tanned skin and an orange complexion. His muscles protrude from his tight shirt. His bald head makes him resemble Mr. Clean. The woman is the opposite, short and frail, her hair in a bun and with deep blue beaded eyes. They both grab me and attempt to hold me in my chair. My body is moving, fighting, biting, but my mind stands still, staring at the ceiling and wondering what the hell is happening.

Blood sprays through the air.

Is it mine or theirs?

I don't know.

Am I crazy?

Am I dreaming?

I don't know.

A needle pierces my arm, and a soothing wave washes over me, unfurling tension from my body like a fading echo. The room, once expansive, now seems to shrink, its dimensions collapsing. I cast a sidelong glance at Dr. Mocker, and an unsettling vision momentarily grips me—a mischievous grin etched upon his face, horns inexplicably sprouting from his head, and a pitchfork held firmly in his hand. I blink and rub my eyes, dispelling the bizarre apparition. Gradually, darkness is all I can see as my body relaxes and my eyelids crush down. Seconds or maybe minutes later, I feel myself being put in a seat and rolled down a hall. I try my hardest to stay awake. My eyes are slightly open as they place me on a bed. I stare at the ceiling until my body and mind sink into the mattress and drift away.

In and out of consciousness, I wonder if this is just a dream. A nightmare I can't awaken from, or maybe purgatory. Maybe I'm being purified before my progression to heaven. Could I have died that night in the cemetery? Perhaps a bullet pierced my heart, my lungs, or a major artery, and now I sit between the living and dead, where I'll suffer for all my transgressions and then journey to heaven. Then again, could all this be hell. Maybe a dream, maybe not. The confusion is overwhelming. I test my hypothesis. With every ounce of strength in my body, I push myself out of bed and run full force toward the white sheetrock wall. More dazed and confused, excruciating pain overcomes me. I fall to the ground as blood runs down my nose.

I'm not dreaming.
This is real!

DEPRESSION

I awaken in this dreary place.

Enclosed in this small room with white walls, hard linoleum flooring, and a hospital bed. It all keeps me in a very depressed state. I wish I were laying in my mahogany king-size canopy bed with its pure white sheets hanging from the palm-tree engraved posts and the soft memory foam mattress. I miss that mattress. It was like sleeping on a cloud, but here, each night, I toss and turn and try to find a spot that relaxes my muscles, but that spot does not exist, so each night, I lay awake wishing, hoping for salvation. I can't quite remember the wish I made to Marie that night, but right now, my only wish is for understanding. I miss my husband. I wish I could hear his voice. I need his guidance. His smooth honey-colored skin, his sweet smile. I need him!

Each thought is so cloudy that it seems as if my mind is in slow motion and my muscles are flaccid. I just don't want to move. Every now and then, I glance out the little window, and all I see are tall dying trees, no flowers or sunshine, just an always-present morning fog. This is not the New Orleans that I love. This is Hell!

I wash my face, brush my teeth, and my hair with my heavy arms and log-tree legs. Each move is forced. Loads of bricks sit on my shoulders and weigh me down. I slowly pull myself back into the bed, letting my body plunk down on the mattress, my head soaking into the pillow. Drifting away, I see myself as a child playing with my brothers and sister. The smell of my mother's blueberry pie circulates under my nose, and my mouth waters for it.

"Watch your brothers and sister," my mom yells out the back door. My brother leaning against the wood-frame shotgun house with his hands over his eyes counting. We run and hide.

"Am I going to wake up?" I ask myself. I know I'm dreaming.

I look up and see the white ceiling of the hospital room, and then I hear my mother saying, "Summer, come walk with me."

Away, I drift, and we walk behind the house. My feet rub across the lush green grass. She takes my hand and says, "He cheated." I look down at my petite frame, my white sundress with red watermelons. I feel my head and touch the two braids and the little hard bows in my hair. "He cheated," I repeat, but this time looking into her sorrow-filled eyes.

Someone moves my arm, cold wetness spreads on the crook of my arm, and I smell alcohol. A quick pain strikes me, and I will myself out of the dream. My eyes open, and I see the blonde nurse's back as she walks toward the room door, a needle in hand. "Wait," I say in a shallow voice, but she doesn't even turn and look my way.

With all the strength my body possesses, I muster one leg out of bed, my foot hits the floor, and then my whole body collapses. I see her white shoes as they turn and walk toward me. "Help," I hear her scream. A pair of black Nikes come through the door toward my weak body. I feel hands lifting me and lying me back in the bed. I try to speak, but before my lips can make out a word, I am back playing with my brothers and sister, my mother in the house baking pies.

Hours pass, and I awaken. A little lucid, I sit up in bed, stretch my arms and legs, and roll my neck from side to side.

How can they say I killed Charles! I loved him!

"I loved him!" I catch myself screaming.

I don't believe them. I could never harm him. He can't be gone. I put protection spells that my mama taught me on everyone close to me. I know he's alive, but maybe someone is setting me up. Tears begin rolling down my cheeks. I stand up, walk to the door of the room, and try to turn the knob, and it's locked. I begin furiously hitting the door, and with bruised hands, I drop onto my knees, screaming, "He's alive, he's alive, I know he's alive!!"

Crying on the cold hard floor, I realize I can't continue to act this way!

I must gain control of myself and figure this out.

I get up off the floor, walk over to a white wood chair in front of a desk, and search my mind for memories. The door to the room opens, and a medium-built Spanish woman with short black hair walks in.

"Is everything okay?"

"Do you know why I'm here?"

"I can't discuss anything with you."

"When will I be able to speak with the doctor again?" I ask her.

"If you behave, you can go to his office after your lunch. Give me a few minutes, and I'll bring you a lunch tray," she says.

I frown.

If I behave, am I a child?

I don't even have the energy to acknowledge her belittling comment.

Within twenty minutes, she returns carrying a tan tray that she lays on the desk in front of me. Then she says, "I'll return in about thirty minutes to get your tray, and I can take you to Dr. Mocker then. I'm in charge for the next ten hours, so if you need something, knock on the door, and I'll hear it and come. By the way, my name is Rosa. As long as you give me no problems, you'll have no problems from me."

I don't respond. On the tray is transparent plastic foil over a plastic plate, a plastic cup with brown liquid, another plastic cup with water, and a small plastic bowl with red Jell-O. I pull the plastic back to fully see meatloaf, mashed potatoes, and green beans. I hate meatloaf, but I'm so hungry I'll eat anything right now. Taking a sip from the brown liquid, I find it's unsweetened tea. I cringe at the strong, brewed flavor. I knew it was tea when I first saw it, but I wish it could be an iced caramel macchiato or French vanilla latte with an extra shot of espresso. Some actual caffeine would have really hit the spot. Sitting, eating the below-standard food, my mind ponders questions to ask the doctor.

Question 1. How was my husband killed?

Question 2. On what day was he killed?

Question 3. Where is my daughter?

Questions 4. Am I allowed to make a phone call, and if so, when?

Question 5. How long will I be in here?

Questions 6. What if I refuse the ECT therapy or whatever it is?

Thoughts flow in my mind, circling my brain, soaring in my spirit. I don't realize how much time has passed until Rosa enters the room. My palms turn a little sweaty and cold as I prepare my mind for another encounter with Dr. Mocker.

We walk to his office in quietness. She knocks on his door, and he greets us as he opens it.

"I'll call you when our session is over," he tells her, and she turns her back and walks away.

"Hello, Summer. Have a seat." He points to the chair in front of his desk.

I sit.

"How are you today?" he asks.

"Deeply depressed," I spit out.

"Why are you deeply 'depressed?'" He makes quotation marks with his fingers. Is he trying to mock me?

Aggravation rises in me, and my bones feel like they want to jump out of my body. I let out a hard exhale before answering, "You, the doctor, why do you think I'm depressed, Mr. Ph.D.?"

"I only want to help you, but you must let me," he says.

A wave of sorrow engulfs me, and my voice falters, words no longer within my reach. My trembling hands instinctively cradle my face as it sags forward, a silent surrender to the weight of despair. The cacophony of questions that once stormed my mind vanishes, replaced by uncontrollable sobs. At this moment, his words, and indeed, all words, hold zero meaning. Life itself feels of no significance. He rises from his seat and walks toward me, his presence casting a long shadow over my anguish. As I gaze downward, my eyes lock onto his brown Louis Vuitton shoes. His fingers slowly lift my chin, and he looks directly into my eyes. His hazel eyes capture a mystic force within my soul. In his eyes, I see brightness, happiness, a person with no pain.

Until now, I hadn't noticed the gentle glow of his skin, the graceful curls that frame his hair, or the captivating aura that envelops his demeanor. He grabs my hand, and for just a few seconds, I feel warmth and comfort. Part of the comfort comes from his grip. It's firm and masculine. For just those seconds, a sense of normality flutters through me. He begins to slowly caress my hand. Is this appropriate? Comes to my mind. But then he speaks.

"I'm here to listen to anything you want to talk about. I'll never pass judgment on you in any way. I only want to help you."

This time, his words are soothing. They enter my body and warm my icicle heart. A small surge of hope pops up in my mind. I begin feeling like my life isn't over, and a quarter of an ounce of grief slips through my soles. We are in complete silence for what seems like hours, but only seconds pass, then minutes, and the tears that once flowed down my face leave behind translucent lines. Dr. Mocker breaks the silence.

"If you want to talk, we can talk. If you want to just sit here, we can also do that."

He walks back to his chair, and we sit in silence. Emotions flow through me, uncertainty, weakness, hatred, desire, hurt, pain, why me, who am I in this bubble of life, what's the purpose of this life, will this sadness ever go away, will I ever know normality again and then the words, "I feel like talking," spit forth from my mouth.

"Good," Dr. Mocker says as he sips his coffee.

"What should I talk about?"

"Have any memories come back?"

"I remember bits and pieces."

"I really want to get to know who Summer James is. How about you tell me about your childhood?"

"Okay, I was born Summer Baptiste. My mother gave birth to me in what the old folks called a shotgun house because if you open the front door and shoot a shotgun, it won't hit anything. It will go straight through and out the back door. Most of the homes in the neighborhood were made like this. I was born and raised right here in the heart of New Orleans, within the Bywater community, a stone's throw from the Mississippi River.

"Dr. Mocker, this is going to sound crazy, but I remember before I was born as well."

"Before you were born? Tell me about it," Dr. Mocker says as if he genuinely cares about what I have to say. In that moment, the simple act of speaking, of sharing my thoughts, feels like a balm to my soul after days spent in silence, enveloped by the suffocating embrace of sadness and suffering.

"I can remember being in a joyous place of warmth, my surroundings illuminated like the sun on a hot summer evening. Happiness and laughter were everywhere. The smell of lilies danced in the air, and Jesus approached my soul, his appearance figureless but brilliant. He asked me if I was willing to travel in physical form one more time. I said yes. He told me he had a purpose for me, but he had to keep it a secret, and when the time came, all would be revealed. That's all of that memory I can remember, but I know it really happened because the memory is so clear and vivid. My mother always told me I was special, but I guess maybe everyone's mother tells their kids that. I also have glimpses of being held by my mother in the hospital, but between then and about four years old, everything fades away until about twelve. Then, the last few years of my life seem distant. Like when you have a brain fog and something you know but you can't seem to remember when asked about it. Does that make any sense to you?"

"It does."

"Do you think it's possible you could have dreamed any of this?" Doctor Mocker asks.

"It's possible, but I believe it happened. I can just feel it. You might think I'm crazy, but I'm not. I consider myself a spiritualist. Are you a religious man, Dr. Mocker?"

"No, I'm not."

"So, what do you believe?"

"I don't believe anything. I just live my life, but this session isn't about me. It's about you."

"Why, the past few days, it seems like I've been in a daze, in and out of consciousness."

"I prescribed you medicine to help you relax."

"It does more than help me relax."

"Summer, do you remember your husband?"

"Absolutely."

"What was your relationship like?"

"I loved my husband. He was my knight in shining armor."

"Did you have a good marriage?"

"As far as I can remember. Do you know who has my daughter right now?"

Dr. Mocker opens a folder on his desk, flips through some pages, stops, reads one of the pages, and closes the folder back.

"Your sister-in-law, Melanie James, has her."

My nose instantly turns up. It's not the best place, but it's better than being in a foster home.

"When can I call her?"

"You can make calls on Tuesdays and Thursdays."

"Do you have a number for her?"

"No, I don't."

"So, how am I supposed to check on my daughter?"

"I'm sorry, Summer, but that's out of my hands."

My foot kicks the bottom of Dr. Mocker's desk, making a loud thump sound.

"Dr. Mocker, how did I supposedly kill him?" A few tears gather in my eyes as I ask the question.

"Summer, I hate to cut you off, but we must stop here. We've actually gone over fifteen minutes. We can pick back up tomorrow if you're up to it. In the meantime, I want you to write as much as possible in this journal. I'm going to decrease your anti-anxiety medicine and increase your anti-depressant's dosage, and hopefully, it will help you to cope with everything that's going on around you."

"But we haven't even been talking about that," I exclaim.

"I'm sorry, but you didn't have an appointment today, and I have other patients who do. I just wanted to make sure you are adjusting after your last procedure."

Dr. Mocker extends a black book toward me, its cover bearing a leather-like texture and graced with a delicate pink flower on the front. As it settles into my hand, an unexpected sense of stability washes over me. In this book, I see a portal to another world, a haven where I can pour my thoughts onto its blank pages and reveal my true feelings. Hopefully, this notebook will be just as relaxing as the pills he prescribes me.

"Thank you, but please, I need to find a way to call my daughter."

"I will see what I can find out for you. I'm also going to take you off restrictions. You'll be able to walk in the hallways by yourself. Starting tomorrow, you can go to the cafeteria to eat or to the dayroom, but you only have access to this floor. Cameras are everywhere, and they are always watching you. It's two security guards who constantly walk the halls of this floor. Other staff members are always around as well. If you do anything you shouldn't, these restrictions will be taken away, and you'll be in your room. Also, the room doors lock at 8:00 PM every evening, and they unlock at 7:00 AM, so these are the times you have to be outside your room. You got it?"

"I got it."

Dr. Mocker calls the nurse to escort me back to my room. She arrives within minutes as if she was close by.

"How was your session?"

"Okay."

"You get off restrictions tomorrow. Are you happy?"

"I guess." I'm really not in the mode for small talk. So many things are circulating in my mind. I Have to figure out how to get my sister-in-law's number so I can check on my daughter. It would mean the world to hear her voice, even if it's just for a second.

We walk down the hospital hall, and I see all the faces of the doctors and nurses of the past in chronological order. As I reach the end, close to the nurses' station, there are pictures of the present hospital staff. The minute I see the image of Dr. Mocker, it sends shivers down my spine. Something is not right, but I can't quite put my finger on it. The picture shows him in a blue suit with a checkered yellow and blue tie, standing next to an American flag. Something about that picture seems so familiar as if I've seen it before. Maybe when they admitted me, I saw it there, and perhaps that's why I get this feeling of deja vu mixed with fear.

Why do I feel fear?

BRUNSWICK BULLIES

Today is the first day I get to eat in the lunchroom. The first week after I awakened from the ECT, they brought food to my room. They say it's procedural to do that to all patients, just to ensure they are not a threat to anyone. Today, they knocked on my door and announced breakfast. I eagerly get up from the bed, get dressed, and walk out the door. In the daytime, they leave our doors unlocked, but at night, staff can come in, but we can't go out. I begin to walk with some others to the lunchroom. The light honeydew-colored walls leading to the lunchroom make the hall look bright and welcoming. I feel excited to be visiting another part of the building. I need a change of scenery. It can feel suffocating to be in the same room for days. Strolling in front of me is three women.

One is short and medium-built. She turns and looks at me. I can feel her green-grape-colored, almond-shaped eyes penetrate my aura. It's as if she looks at me angrily and then quickly turns away, but how could she? She doesn't know me. The tallest of the bunch looks like a model. She has to be at least six feet or 6'1, about 150 pounds, with blonde hair and blue eyes—a tall version of Samantha from Bewitched. The woman closest to her is at least a foot shorter, medium build, short brown hair, and thick eyebrows growing together. Something about her makes me shiver. The three women chat continuously, looking back and giggling every few seconds like schoolhouse girls. Loneliness circulates my bones. Keeping to myself the past few days really depressed me. There has never been a time that I didn't have someone to talk to.

Entering the lunchroom, it resembles a medium-sized Luby's or Piccadilly restaurant. There are lots of round tables with chairs. Each table has a vase with artificial flowers resting on its surface. On one side of the room, people are standing in line, waiting for the staff to place their selections on their plates. Desperately following the group of women, I stand behind them, hoping maybe they'll invite me to sit at their table. This reminds me of when I was a teenager, and my mom took me away from my friends and put me in a new school filled with strangers. Loneliness, depression, and pain became my unwelcome companions, blurring my sense of self-confidence. Eating lunch alone, navigating the foreign halls by myself, and now here I am, an adult experiencing the same torture. My breath leaves my body and I tell myself "inhale, exhale, inhale, exhale. Everything is okay. I'm okay." I take the food tray, close my eyes for a second, and my breathing returns.

The selection of food is pretty average. They have everyday carbohydrate-heavy foods like pancakes, biscuits with gravy, and French toast. I skip all that and move toward the proteins: eggs and bacon. I refuse to let my figure go, regardless of where I am. After filling my tray and getting a cup of orange juice, I walk around the dining room, looking for the women I was walking behind. I see them sitting at a table in the back of the room. Taking a deep breath, I begin walking toward their table. They appear to be in deep conversation.

The medium-built woman with short brown hair glances my way and looks at me with a scrunched-up face. The closer I get, the more I begin to realize they must be talking about me. I pass up their table and sit at another nearby. The inside of my body starts to heat up, and the hairs on my arms stand erect, a feeling I get whenever someone is staring at me. I turn and look in the women's direction; sure enough, their eyes are on me.

"Are Brunswick Bullies bothering you again?" I turn back to see an oversized, pale, freckled-faced woman holding a tray.

"Brunswick Bullies?" I reply.

"Are you okay, Summer?" the woman asks me.

"You know me."

"Of course, I know you," she says as she sits in front of me.

"We always sit together." She looks confused.

"We do?"

"I'm sorry. Can you tell me your name?"

"Whitney."

The woman begins to eat her food very fast. Something seems very odd about her, but everything has been weird lately, so I put it to the back of my mind and begin to eat my food. A plastic salt shaker sits on the table. I grab it, twist the lid off, pour some in my hand, and throw it over my left shoulder.

"My mother used to do that. She would say it brings her luck," Whitney says.

I burst into laughter, and it feels so good to laugh. Whitney looks at me and tilts her head to the side.

"I'm sorry, it's just that my mother used to say the same thing, and I really don't believe it, but I have a habit of doing it."

"Mothers and superstitions," Whitney says.

"Are we friends?" I ask her.

"We most certainly are."

Whitney smiles at me, and the smile looks pretty pure and genuine. An array of warm energy and good vibes bounces off Whitney.

"I'm sorry, I don't remember you, but I had something called ECT done, and the doctor says sometimes it temporarily takes your memory away."

"It's okay. It's not the first time you forgot who I was."

"I hope it's the last," I tell her.

It's awkward sitting next to someone who is supposed to be your friend, and you have no idea who they are.

"You know, Summer, we have a lot in common, and that's why we're friends."

"Like what?"

"We were both raised by very spiritual mothers, and we both believe in the great power of Marie Laveau."

"But I don't practice any of that stuff like my mother did," I tell Whitney.

"I know, but that doesn't mean Marie doesn't watch over you. She does, and she told me to tell you to look toward your dreams for answers."

"What?" I ask, puzzled.

Whitney stuffs the last of her food in her mouth.

"It was nice seeing you today. I missed you and our conversations. I'm going to my room now. I'll see you around," she tells me as she gets up with her tray and walks away.

Standing up, I walk toward Whitney to ask her if she knows anything about why I'm in here, but the tall, blonde, slender woman from the group Brunswick Bullies approaches me and grabs my arm.

"Ignore her. She's crazy," the lady says with a backwoods drawl as she looks toward Whitney. She intertwines my arm with hers and begins walking me down the hall.

"I didn't empty my tray," I tell her.

"Honey, don't worry. That's what these workers get paid for," she says while pointing to one of the cafeteria staff.

"I'm Paula. My friends and I saw you talking to Whitney. I figured I would come to save you. She crazy as a Betsy bug, worse than the rest of us." I don't know what to say, so I say nothing; I just listen. We walk over to her friends, who appear extremely happy and giggly. Yet, nothing but negativity seems afloat in the air. They peer at me and smile.

Paula drops my arm. "So, you murdered your husband, hon. Was he awake or asleep?" Paula asks with a sadistic, monstrous smile on her face. Strength leaves my body, my legs become lifeless, falling to the ground, and I can no longer move. I sit on the floor, my knees curling up to my chest in a ball. The woman, Paula, continues walking and begins laughing. Her friends get up from their table and follow in pursuit.

Once again, I'm on the cold, hard floor, and I don't know if I can get up this time. My mind tells me to stand, but anxiety whirls around in my body like a category four hurricane. Katrina hit again, spinning around my mind, drenching my soul with sharp stabs of affliction. To hear the damning accusation of murdering your own husband struck a blow to my heart. Love and affection are all my heart feels and has ever felt for Charles. The thought of myself harming him rips me apart. He was the love of my life. My soulmate, the very essence of my joy and completeness.

"It's okay, get up. Don't let them get the best of you." The words slowly and quietly enter my ears; no one stands next to me, so I'm unsure where they are coming from, but they bring slivers of internal calmness and strength with them. I stand, dust myself off, and begin walking out of the cafeteria, not paying attention to the eyes watching my actions. A short, frail nurse with curly blonde hair approaches me.

"Summer, is everything okay?" she asks me with a northern, probably New York, accent. New Orleans has such a melting pot of people here.

"I'm fine."

"I saw you on the floor. Are you sure you're okay? Did you fall?"

"Yes, I'm fine. I'm just heading back to my room."

"It's actually preferred that patients go to the day room during the day. You can meet some of the other patients, and usually, they have games going on and TV time."

"I would prefer to go to my room."

"Okay. I just want you to know it's not good to be anti-social," she says in a condescending tone. If the 'Brunswick Bullies' are what I've got to look forward to in the dayroom, I think I'll be spending the majority of my time in my room.

NIGHTTIME

The day soars by and turns to evening, then night. With the sun's descent, the sky transforms from a canvas of magnificent pinkish orange and banana berry blue hues to a shroud somber of gray-black darkness. Night casts its shadow, and everyone is expected to fall asleep. I hate sleep; my heart is closed to sleep! When we die, we sleep forever. Why must we sleep now? Why couldn't there be another way to rest our bodies? Laying in my bed, I stare at the ceiling, daydreaming and fantasizing, wishing I was a mythical creature with magical powers, like a vampire that could live forever. I would travel the world without any care, visiting famous cities and monuments across the globe, like the Sistine Chapel in the Vatican or the pyramids in Egypt. My heart would stray from love, and my mind would open to the cultures of the world. Sleep slowly creeps up on me as I fantasize, and as the minutes pass, my thoughts slow down. I eventually fall asleep, but it's not intentional.

Hours of no dreams and a light doze pass by until I'm awakened to the feeling of being watched. Nervousness passes throughout my body, and I just lay there still as if I had never awakened. Sometimes, I see things and never know if they are real or fake, so I ignore them, and they disappear. This is not going away. Could this be a phony apparition, my mind once again playing a cruel joke on me? The thin white sheet that covers me begins easing down.

Now, this is new.

Never before have any of the things I've seen moved anything. The sheet stops right below my breast. A hand touches and then caresses my right breast. The sound of breathing and a faint heartbeat runs through my ears, bringing sound to the deadly, quiet room. I sit up, uneasiness, apprehension, and darkness surrounding me, along with the vague shadow figure that stands next to my bed.

Quickly, I stand. The figure freezes as my feet hit the ice-cold floor, but my determination is not deterred, and I run over to the bathroom, pushing the door open and turning on the light. As the brightness fills the air, chasing out darkness, my eyes automatically close for a second too long, and I can hear the sound of the door closing. Whoever had entered my room is now gone. I run over to the bedroom door and turn the knob.

"Of course, it's locked."

They lock the doors at night, so we can't wander the halls. Staff can enter, but we can't exit. With no choice but to climb back into bed, I leave the bathroom light on and hope the pervert who entered my room does not return. I lie there for hours, frantic and too scared to fall back asleep. Drowsiness weaves through the crevices of my mind, but the adrenaline in my body kicks it away. Fuzzy, blurry thoughts of my husband enter, moving through my heart like a worm in a plum.

None of this seems real.

Thinking back, I can remember the sandalwood, citrus, and bergamot smell of his cologne. I would lay my head on his chest and run my fingers through his curly hair while we lay in bed. It's funny so many people would walk up to him and start speaking Spanish because of his dark complexion and curly hair; they thought he was Dominican. We always joked about it. We would talk in bed for hours. He was my best friend. The love of my life, more than just a husband, we were family. We practically grew up together. It's no way I would harm him. I just don't believe it's possible. I kind of wonder if there was something he could have done to make me want to hurt him? The only thing I can think of is if he tried to harm our daughter, and I couldn't imagine that. He was the best father ever. A better parent than me, always there, always showing love. It's crazy for me to even think he would harm her.

Wiping my tears away on the stiff, starched sheets, sleep tortures me like an annoying fly, easing upon me and then slipping away before I can catch it. Boredom echoes my surroundings, intertwining with sleep. I open up my journal and begin to write. Although my mind is empty, words move through my limbs and into the pen that strokes the paper. I have no idea what the words are—I just let them fly.

Within minutes, my pen gives up its fight to write, and in a sign of defeat, it falls to the journal, making a clamping noise. The journal slightly folds its pages, showing off the victory, but sleep is the true victor. It appears, it tortures, it defeats, and now it's sweeping my mind away.

Easing into a dream so vivid and clear, the midnight moon dances across the sky. Grayish clouds romance each other against the moonlight's shadow. I lie on my back in the midnight breeze, sucking in the fresh smell of roses and lilies. I know this is a dream, but I indulge in it. Crickets chirp in the grass. Silence floating on the surface of the earth. I bathe in the simplicity of life, riding the wave of peace and relaxation. I forget the place I've arrived at and let my mind soak in solitude. Here I now lie somewhere in between sleep and wake. I hear the footsteps in the hallway by the door, but at the same time, I hear the howl of a wolf echoing in the air. This dream becomes my peace, my haven from the world. My heart opens to the night, and I drift to a deeper sleep and more vivid dream. I arrive in a cemetery at the foot of Marie Laveau's tomb. Overgrown grass surrounds the area, and tall above-ground tombs encompasses the space. Her tomb is covered in X's, surrounded by flowers and burning candles. "Grant me a wish, grant me a wish," I whisper under my breath as I drop to the ground.

A medium-built, light complexion beautiful woman of color appears next to me as I lay on the ground weeping. She squats down and starts running her fingers through my hair. I look in her beautiful mystical eyes. Warmth, love, and happiness flow down my body. My eyes open wide. I smile, I smile a big smile because I'm so happy to be in the presence of love in human form. Marie's spirit feels like joy, freedom, and encouragement. She whispers in my ear, "Summer, you must talk to Whitney. She can help you. Ask her for her help. Stay away from those other women."

"Help me how?" I try to ask, but as the words roll from my lips, conciseness takes over, and sleep leaves me to evade another body.

My eyelids roll open, and another shadow figure stands by the room door, staring at me. The fear in my heart creates courage, balling my fists. I will not be touched again. The light switch flips on, and the same tall, slim woman with dreads that I encountered on the first day stands there, holding a plastic cup of water and a pill cup. Without any words, she hands them to me, and I comply. She leaves the room, and I drift back to sleep, this time with no dreams, just a deep, deep, soothing sleep.

Take me back, Marie.

Hours pass, and the morning light invades the room. The sound of a plethora of footsteps oozes from under the threshold. A knock on the door sends my spirit spiraling from my body like a yo-yo.

"Breakfast," a voice yells through the room door. I immediately get out of bed and head to the door.

"Excuse me," I say to the same woman from last night. She turns and looks at me with great disdain. It's apparent she doesn't like me.

What's up her ass, I wonder.

"Yes?" she says with a roll of her eyes. Looking down, I spot her name tag. Delisa.

"Someone came into my room last night," I tell her.

"I was on duty all last night, and I can assure you no one walked into your room," she says as she rolls her neck, turns, and walks away. That woman has issues, and you mean to tell me she worked all last night and is still here? With all the overtime she does, she could have easily fallen asleep when someone came into my room. I look down and notice I'm in the middle of the hall in my nightgown. Running to my room, I hop back into bed. My body feels so sluggish, and my muscles and stomach ache as if I have a hangover. All my thoughts seem to meld together. The medication they give me swipes my energy.

I just want to lay in bed all day, but my mind keeps thinking about Whitney. I must talk to her. I get back out of bed, slowly wash my face, brush my teeth, and put my hair up in a little bun. Why are my movements dragging? My selection of clothing is minimal. They are definitely different from the clothes I would have packed for myself. I must remember to ask Dr. Mocker who brought these clothes for me. I pick a purple tank top and some black yoga pants. I take the comfort route, and plus, all I have is tennis shoes, so I refuse to wear one of these flowery sundresses with tennis shoes.

Leaving the room, a million questions for Dr. Mocker and Whitney race through my mind. I begin thinking about the different pills they give me. One of the nurses administers a white pill shaped like a bar with three scores twice a day. From day one, I knew that pill was clouding my mind, so I've been hiding it under my tongue. Once they turn their head or look the other way, I spit it in my hand and flush it down the toilet when I go to my room, but Delisa always asks me to open my mouth and raise my tongue.

One of the nurses, Barry, never watches to see if I take the pills, so I just put the ones he gives me in my pocket. I've been saving them—for what, I'm unsure, but I just figure they might come in handy one day. Whenever I don't take the pills, I have such clear thoughts. Pieces of my memory are still missing, but I feel the memories will soon return. They must.

As soon as I bend the corner to go down the hall toward the dining room, I spot one of Brunswick Bullies. Taking a deep breath, I continue on my path without looking in her direction. Apparently, no matter where you are, there are mean and rude people. I get to the double glass doors of the dining room and peer in, hoping to catch a glimpse of Whitney before I enter, but I don't see her.

Paula, one of the Brunswick Bullies, approaches, and instead of moving to avoid me, she walks right into me.

"Excuse you," I say, my voice barely audible.

"What did you say, husband killer?"

"Has anyone ever told you, that you're a total bitch, like with a capital B," I tell her.

"I can tell they have you on some heavy medication, so I'm going to let your silly comments slide, but next time, you might not be so lucky," Paula tells me as she opens the glass doors and enters the dining room. I see the third member of her squad sitting at a table, looking my way. Without much of an appetite, I debate whether or not to even go in, but I can't starve myself. I should eat something, so I go ahead and enter through the doors. Once inside, the smell of the food guides me like Toucan Sam. I follow my nose, my stomach growls, and my appetite says, "Here I am. Feed me." I glaze upon a large assortment of divine-smelling breakfast delicacies.

Food has an effect on me. It makes me excited and happy when I'm sad. When I was younger, I was overweight and would eat sweets all day until the doctor told my mom I was on the verge of diabetes. She began mixing up herbs and making me drink all kinds of disgusting potions until I no longer had an appetite. The weight started to fall off my body. Once I stopped drinking her mixtures, the weight began to come back, and it's been up to me to have healthy eating habits, but Charles loved my size. I once heard his friend call him a chubby chaser and I would always tease him and say, "You like fat girls, huh." He was my knight in shiny armor. He saved me from myself. Not many men would have put up with my bipolar attitude, depression, and mood swings, but he was always there to pick me up when I was down.

The smell of the fresh pancakes put an automatic smile on my face, but I look away and tell myself, "I am discipline. I am discipline." I decide on yogurt, a banana, and a glass of orange juice. I walk with my tray, looking for a table, and none of the tables are empty, so I approach an older lady with white hair who seems harmless. I ask if I can sit by her. She gazes up and stares at me for a few seconds, then says, "Sure, baby, go ahead and have a seat."

I set my tray down, peeling back the foil from my blueberry yogurt, and she just stares at me. I figure I'll continue and pretend I don't notice her stare.

"You, Summer?" she asks.

"Yes, ma'am," I reply. Her stare continues.

"Do you know Whitney?" I ask her.

"Everybody knows Whitney," she says and continues to look at me.

"Do you know where she is?"

"She's probably in her room. She was right about you," she says.

"Right about me? What did she say about me?" I ask.

"You're special." As she says that, I look up from my yogurt, and that's when I notice her pale face, birdy eyes, narrow nose, and thin, ruby painted lips. She's the woman I saw before staring at the wall.

"How am I special?" Tears begin to run down the lady's face. She picks up her tray and walks away.

What just happened? Is everyone in this place crazy? I'm probably the only sane person here besides the nurses and the doctors, and they probably have problems, too. I begin trying to rationalize that whole conversation when a tall attractive guy walks up.

"Can I sit here?" he asks.

"Sure. Just finishing up," I tell him.

"You don't have to rush. There's enough room at the table."

I laugh. "I'm sorry, I'm just a little on edge," I tell him. This man is gorgeous. Why haven't I noticed him before? I glance up at his green eyes and shoulder-length, brownish-black dreads. Then I look away. I don't want to be a starer like that other woman.

"What's your name?" I ask him.

"Eric," he says with a smile. I smile back.

"I noticed Sandra got up crying," he says.

"Who?" I reply.

"Sandra, the lady that was sitting here with you."

"Oh, she never told me her name, but yes, she started crying for no reason and left."

"She does that from time to time. She's a very sweet old lady but extremely emotional," he tells me.

"Do you know Whitney?"

"Whitney is cool. I talk to her all the time in passing. From what I've heard, she has a sixth sense, somewhat like a psychic. She can tell your past and future. She even knows how people are feeling."

I interrupt Eric and ask, "How long has she been here?"

"She has definitely been here longer than me, and I've been here a year. She keeps to herself, and personally, I think that's a good thing. There are some crazy people in here who can make your life hell. Trust me."

As he finishes his sentence, he looks over at the table with Paula and her friends. They seem to be engaged in a funny conversation because all three are laughing.

"A year? How long do people stay in here?"

"It all depends on what you're in for."

"What do you know about Dr. Mocker?" I ask Eric.

"He's not my doctor, but I hear he's good. He's actually the director of the place, and he only has a very small number of patients. Usually, only the real nut jobs have him as a doctor. Why do you ask?"

"I guess I'm one of the nut jobs," I reply to Eric. His face turns crimson.

"I-I-I'm sorry," he stutters.

"It's okay. You're not the first to call me a nut job, and you probably won't be the last."

We both laugh.

"Dr. Mocker's a good doctor, from what I hear. What he says carries weight around here. He's friends with all the judges, and if you want any chance of getting out, you want to be on his good side," Eric tells me.

"I'll keep that in mind."

I glance at the huge oval-shaped clock on the wall and realize I have ten minutes to get to my session with Dr. Mocker.

"Speaking of the doctor, I have an appointment with him in a few minutes," I tell Eric as I get up from the table and grab my tray.

Unlike Paula, I think it's rude and lazy to just leave your tray on the table when you're supposed to dump it. Why create extra work for the staff? They probably only get minimum wage. I dump my tray and begin walking toward the cafeteria doors. Glancing ahead,

I see the Brunswick Bullies and dread passing them. They seem to be evil beings and need to be avoided, but their table is right next to the exit, and the closer I get, the more they giggle and look my way.

Focusing my gaze ahead, trying to relax and ignore their giggles, I walk beside their table. Right before I can fully pass, I feel my leg hitting someone else's. I lose my balance and begin falling to the ground. My hands reach down to try to break my fall, but somehow, I fall directly on top of my arm. Immediately, the impact sends pain striking up from my hand to my shoulder. Ice-cold reddish liquid, probably cranberry juice, falls on top of my head, rolling down my hair and onto my face.

Glancing up, I see Paula holding an empty cup. Laughter surrounds me, and all I want to do is cower. Even Delisa is standing by the juice bar at the front of the room, laughing. Tears gather in the corners of my eyes, but I suppress them with all my might. Eric appears by my side in seconds and grabs me by the arm to help me up. He dusts scrambled eggs off my shirt that I must have landed in. Laughter is vibrating throughout the entire room. Eric hands me a bunch of napkins, and I wipe the sticky juice off my face, dabbing around my eyes to get any moisture or wetness that may have seeped out from the corners.

"Better be careful, Paula. She's a killer," says one of the evil bullies sitting at the table.

"What is she going to do? Kill me, too?" Paula says, full of laughter.

"What is this high school! Y'all are acting horribly. Mature some, please!" Eric yells at them.

I gain my composure and begin walking out of the cafeteria with Eric by my side. Some people can really be bad human beings. Even outside the room, we can still hear laughter.

"Paula can be a total bitch. Try to ignore her," Eric tells me loud enough for them to hear.

"I hate her! She's such a horrible person! She's behaving like a high school teenager. Someone needs to teach her a lesson."

"I agree," says Eric.

"Thanks for helping me up."

"It was nothing. Would you like for me to walk you to your room?"

"No, I just want to be alone for a few minutes, but thanks."

"Catch you later," Eric says as he turns and walks back toward the cafeteria.

There's no way I'm going to make it to Dr. Mocker's office by my appointment time. My hair lays limp on my neck, and the sides of my face and neck feel icky and sticky from the juice. A shower is imperative right now.

SESSION WITH
DR. MOCKER

Two days go by before I'm able to get another appointment with Dr. Mocker. I've learned to stay to myself and spend all my free time in my room. My daily routine is showering, going to breakfast, then back to my room, going to lunch, dinner, and then back to my room again. Some days I see Whitney in passing, but most days, I don't. Eric is always entertaining when I sit with him, but for the most part, I'm a loner.

The variety of people that surround me ranges from extremely deranged to extremely sad and depressed. Getting caught up in the wrong conversation can cause your entire day to go horribly wrong. One conversation with a guy, which I thought would be a good exchange, turned sinister when he started talking about his love of little children and the sickening things he likes to do with them. His unsettling confessions about an attraction to children, an affliction he struggled with since he was a teenager, sent shivers down my spine. They expect us to talk to each other and socialize, but when you're normal, and everyone else is crazy, it's impossible.

I approach Dr. Mocker's office and gently knock on his door. The camera peers down at me. I wonder who watches these cameras. Maybe they are decoys.

Dr. Mocker opens the door. "Come in and have a seat," he says while holding the door open for my passage.

Behind his desk, above the numerous diplomas and certificates, are three huge windows showering the room with bright afternoon light. The light brings warmth and comfort to the cold air-conditioned room. I sit in the chair across from his desk. Today must be causal Friday because he's dressed in jeans that hug his butt and a tight navy polo that rubs against his chest, revealing his pectoral muscles.

"How are you today?" he asks me.

"I'm surviving."

"What exactly does that mean?"

"I'm here, and I can't do anything about it, so I'm surviving, trying to make the best out of a dreadful situation."

Dr. Mocker walks over to his swivel tobacco-colored leather chair, takes a seat, and begins writing in a notebook.

"Are you beginning to remember what happened?"

"No."

"Let's start with talking about your life from where we left off, and you can tell me as much as you remember. When things start getting foggy, we will try to figure them out."

"First, I need you to answer some of my questions. When do I get a phone call?"

"We try to give patients one phone call every week, but it's a courtesy, and sometimes it's possible you may not receive a phone call."

"Well, I haven't received a phone call."

"I'll make sure you get your call."

"I would really like to talk to my daughter."

"You'll get your call."

"Thank you. Now, can you tell me what happened to my husband? How was he murdered?"

Dr. Mocker straightens his glasses and pulls them close to his nose. It must be a nervous habit because he's always doing that.

"It's reported that your husband was stabbed multiple times, then a fire was set to your home, burning his body."

I swallowed, but the dryness of my mouth didn't allow me to take anything down. I'm very visual, so to hear it is to see it in my mind. Sitting in the hard-cushioned chair, my mind spirals. Thoughts of Charles's body lying on the ground, stabbed and then burnt with fire. His handsome face covered with black flakes, revealing an ash-stained skull.

"Are you okay, Summer? Do you need a drink of water?"

I begin thinking back to the day my husband and I met, the day we got married, that night when he looked me in my eyes and told me he loved me and was happy he married me. His touch was so tender and soft, he caressed me and kissed every inch of my body that night, making gentle slow love to me then holding me in his arms and telling me that I was the best decision of his life. He swore to love me forever and never let anything or anyone get in between us.

Charles was the kind of man who brightened even the most ordinary of days, surprising me with flowers on a random Monday or leaving a Snickers, my favorite chocolate, on my pillow as I awoke. His thoughtfulness and love were boundless, and he belonged solely to me. It was a love that melted my heart then and still does to this day. Yet, he's no longer a part of this world, and the reality of his absence feels surreal. I yearn to hear his voice, to speak to him, but it remains an unattainable wish.

The day our beautiful baby girl was born seems like yesterday. He rushed me to the hospital and they had to perform an emergency c-section because my blood pressure was so high. Charles stood there dressed in his scrubs. He squeezed my hand so hard, I felt like it was going to break as they cut my stomach. The moment they lifted her up, the biggest smile I had ever seen him possess came across his face. I just wanted to hug and kiss him. At that very moment, I surrendered every ounce of love my body possessed to him. Memory after memory invades my thoughts and stabs my heart with a double-edged sword. It hurts. It feels as if my core was pulled out and shredded to pieces. How am I supposed to get through this!

"Summer, are you okay?"

I look up at the doctor with tearful eyes. "We were supposed to grow old together."

Guilt runs through my veins. Here I am, thinking about how tight the jeans fit on this doctor, and my husband is gone.

"Dr. Mocker, I feel beyond words right now. Did I really kill him?"

"I don't know, Summer, but that's what's in the police reports. You haven't admitted anything to me since you been here."

"What do the police reports say? I need more details. None of this make any sense!"

"I'll give you more details later but for now I want you to focus on remembering."

"Why later?"

He hands me a Kleenex, and I wipe the pouring snot from my nose. Each tear that runs down my cheek feels like a tear of sadness but relief. Why am I feeling relief? I love him. Or I guess it's past tense now. I loved him. What's this relief?

Dr. Mocker drops his pen on the desk and walks over to me. He puts his hand on my back, and softly, like a whisper, he tells me, "You'll get through this." My head falls against the hard crease of his pants, and he rubs my back in a circular motion.

"Everything is going to be okay. You just have to take it a day at a time."

"And what about the details," I persist.

"We will discuss it in time, for now I want you to try to remember as much as you can. I don't want any details to cloud what comes back to you and your narrative become what I tell you."

Dr. Mocker bends down and wraps his arms around me. I hadn't realized it before, but I needed this comfort. My skin goes from cold with goosebumps to warm and sweaty. The tears stop running down, and for the moment, I feel alive. The walls disappear, the building disappears, and nothing exists but me and the comforting touch of this psychiatrist. Human touch is so powerful!

After dinner, I once again skip dayroom activities and adjourn to my room. When I first arrived here, the weather was rainy and dreary, the skies always seemed gray and cloudy, but the skies have since begun to brighten up. The sun has pierced through the crisp clouds, and the window in my room has become my peephole to the world. I see new patients arriving. Some look disorderly and unkempt, some pushed in wheelchairs, drugged, and unconscious to the world, and I've seen others arrive looking perfectly normal in neat attire, walking and talking as if they are walking into a shopping mall or grocery store, except they have handcuffs on their hands or straitjackets wrapped around their bodies.

The hospital parking lot is a spectacle of contrasts, a visual narrative of the medical world's diverse inhabitants. The doctors, in their luxurious BMWs and Mercedes, displays an air of affluence that cling to their sleek cars and spacious SUVs. Nurses, ever practical, rely on trusty Hondas and Toyotas, their reliable steeds carrying them through the rigors of each shift. The security personnel, on the other hand, exhibit a distinct penchant for robust, off-road machines. Ford F-150s with oversized tires and rugged Jeep Wranglers, poised to tackle any terrain, testaments to their vehicular preferences. Amidst this automotive symphony, a motley crew of staff members navigate the lot in vehicles that appeared as if they might sputter their last breath upon ignition.

It quickly became evident that the hospital's security force, touted as an imposing presence, doesn't quite live up to the image they project. The majority are out of shape and look like they'll probably let us go for a donut. From my vantage point by the window, I observe this daily automotive parade, a continuous spectacle that unfolds like a well-rehearsed drama. Each shift change brings forth a new ensemble of healthcare warriors, their comings and goings governed by disparate schedules. Nurses and security guards soldiered through grueling 12-hour shifts, while the doctors, their roles no less demanding, are often bound by 8-hour commitments. Yet, the shortage of physicians sometimes have them to extend their tenure, with a few dedicated souls pushing the envelope to a taxing 16-hour marathon. This window is my television—Channel 5 news. I love shift change. It's amazing what you can learn from watching people for only a few minutes.

The smokers are often seen huddled in designated corners, their puffs of smoke mingling with early morning air. These are the ones who have burned the midnight oil, fortified by the electrifying embrace of Red Bull, as they brace themselves for the day ahead. Then, there are the diligent souls, meticulously attired, their attire pristine, their skirts super straight, and their hair meticulously coiffed. These individuals are staunch advocates of punctuality and compliance, their commitment to their work unflinching.

Lastly, there are those who choose to shed their wedding rings before stepping onto the hospital's hallowed grounds, their reasons known only to them. It's a kaleidoscope of behaviors and quirks that paint a vibrant portrait of the hospital's staff. I just observe and laugh to myself until the skies darken and my window, that's like my television turns off for the night.

Lying in bed, I think about my session with Dr. Mocker and how comforting it was. He's such a caring doctor. His wife is a lucky woman to have such a caring husband.

Crrrr...Crrrr.

What is that?

I awaken by a terrible noise spilling forth from the bathroom door, so I look toward the darkened area. Squinting my eyes, they slowly adjust to the light seeping from under the bedroom door. The brass hinges and the wooden door unfolds before me. Seconds pass, maybe even minutes, and the noise grows faint and disappears. It's probably my dilapidating mind and its trickery games.

Wouldn't be the first time. My mind traveled down a darkened path, down the rabbit hole, and through the woods, to grandma's house I go.

Or it could have been these little bar-shaped pills Delisa gave me before bed, their influence cast a shadow over my consciousness.

I ease back down on the rock-hard mattress and snuggle with the stiff covers, trying to find the exact spot that had catered to my sleep.

Bam! Bam! Bam! The bathroom door opens and closes rapidly— adrenaline surges through my body. I pull the covers tightly to my chest and just lay there, too scared to react. Bam! The door slams close. I jump out of bed and race to the bedroom door without hesitation.

"Open this door," I shout while vigorously banging on it.

I hear the clicking noise and exit the room, bolting down the corridor to the nurse's station.

"Someone is in my room," I yell.

The nurse smacks her gum and looks at me with her head tilted to the side.

"No one is in your room," she says.

"I heard something in the bathroom, and the door opened and closed by itself."

"Okay. Let's go check it out."

"I'm not going in there!" I tell her.

She mumbles a laugh to herself. I really dislike Delisa! I can tell she looks down on me and she walks around here like she has a stick up her ass; maybe not a stick, a log! You know the ugly girl that's mean to you because you're pretty. Well, Delisa is that ugly girl.

"Come on, we can check your room together. I want you to see that no one is in there," she says.

I inhale, then exhale a loud breath, trying to calm my nerves. I follow behind her as she enters the room and flips on the light.

"Check the bathroom," I tell her.

She glares at me and then walks to the bathroom. She flips the light switch on. "Come look," she screams at me while rolling her eyes.

We peer inside and see the porcelain toilet and the white plastic shower curtain with black-speckled, mildewed layered on it.

"Told you, no one is here. Now lay down and get some rest. Probably just a bad dream," she says with sarcasm and a smirk.

The lights suddenly start flashing on and off, and then the room turns dark. Coldness dominates the air. I shiver as the hairs on the back of my neck stand erect. My heart palpitates, and fear circulates in my bloodstream. The darkness masquerades my sight as I run over to the wall. My hand moves against the smooth paint, trying to locate the switch. I feel the rectangular block and begin flipping the switch up and down. The lights remain off.

"Stoppppp," the nurse shrieks.

I run out of the room and into the hallway, terrified. The nurse follows, ramming into me and knocking me to the floor.

Hope they got that on camera.

"You choked me, you crazy woman. What is wrong with you?" she muffles as she holds her neck.

"No, it wasn't me," I try telling her while getting up off the floor. She briskly walks behind the nurse's station, grabs the phone, and dials a number.

"I need assistance and the doctor on staff for tonight. Summer James assaulted me," she tells the person on the other line.

What?

"I didn't touch you," I try telling the nurse as I walk toward her. She steps back.

"Get away from me! I don't want you near me!" she says, still holding her neck.

I stop in my tracks.

"I'm just trying to tell you it wasn't me! Someone else had to be in there with us!"

She waves her hand as if dismissing me. Two orderlies and a security guard approach.

"What's going on?" a tall, slim but muscular security guard named Buck asks.

"That crazy thing there tried to kill me. She choked me," says Delisa.

"No, I didn't," I exclaim to Buck.

"You go to your room," he yells at me.

"No, I'm not going back in there."

"To your room! Now!" he demands.

"No!"

The guard grabs my arm and tries to pull me toward the room. I snatch my arm, run, and sit in one of the old white wicker chairs.

This is crazy.

"Get the haloperidol with promethazine," an orderly named John, who resembles Chris Farley, tells the nurse.

"Did Dr. Mocker authorize that for her?" the nurse replied.

"It's been in her chart to use as needed ever since she had that breakdown," John replies.

Adrenaline surges through my veins, and I immediately jump out of my seat and run down the hall. The coldness of the tile slaps against my feet. Donald, the other orderly, and Buck chase after me; John wobbles. I can feel my heart rate rising and my breathing increasing.

I'm out of shape but it doesn't slow me down. I pass the closed doors that line the hall, unsure of where to go next.

I turn a corner and run into large steel ward doors. I pull on them. *Damn, they're locked. Of course they're locked!*

Beside the doors stands a small Ficus plant. I pick it up and throw it toward the men. The plant lands right in front of them, and John trips on it and falls. Donald and Buck jump over it and continue to run toward me. Immediately, I begin swinging my fists.

If they get me, they are going to sedate me and put me back in that room.

Summoning every ounce of strength, I deliver a fierce punch to Buck's nose, crimson rivulets instantly staining his freckled face. Donald, ever the opportunist, seizes my arm, but my desperation is boundless. A swift, unhesitant kick to his groin sends him recoiling, gasping in agony as he relinquishes his grip. I run back down the hall. Up from his fall, John catches up to me and tasers me. A torrent of electric torment surges through my body. Agonized cries involuntarily escape my lips as my legs betray me, crumpling beneath the relentless assault.

As I sprawl on the unforgiving linoleum floor, convulsions wrack my body, an unrelenting storm of pain surging through every nerve. Fuzzy, disjointed thoughts meander through my beleaguered mind. Through the haze, I glance upward, greeted by the grim spectacle of the men and Delisa looming over me. Delisa's malevolent grin, reminiscent of the Grinch, betrays her sinister delight in my suffering.

With an air of authority, she removes the lid from a needle, plunging it into my arm with a chilling finality.

"Take her to her room," she commands, her voice a chilling decree as I struggle against the darkness descending upon me. The will to resist burning fiercer than ever before, but my body betrays me . "Take her to her room," she says authoritatively.

Warmth from the shot flows through my veins, warming my body as my twitching muscles begin to relax. I see a wheelchair . . . they lift me . . . they place me in it. I try to hit and kick but every limb starts feeling super heavy. Tears slowly come down my cheeks.

What just happened here? My mind dwindling.

"Why did she choke you?" I hear Buck ask the nurse.

"She's erratic."

I try to muster up the strength to join their conversation...

I'm not crazy.

But my dry mouth refuses to move. I hold my peace as they push me to my room. They lay me on the hard mattress and ice cube sheets. My mind slowly climbs the stairs of each forming thought.

What was that noise coming from the bathroom? Was that nurse really choked?

I feel good, relaxed, calm.

I stare at the ceiling, watching the popcorn texture dance before me.

I know I didn't choke . . . why is it so cold . . . I feel so tired. I didn't choke her.

My thoughts run together as the sandman guides me to rest. I let go, and my dreams take over.

I'm dreaming, I know, and it's so lovely here. The sweet smell of my mommy's apple pie is roaming through the air, circulating my nostrils, calling my appetite. The beautiful pink and white lilies and golden azaleas sway with the light breeze off the Mississippi River. The flowers flavor the air with their sweet honey fragrance. I'm a child again, running with my brothers and sister. We chase each other on this cool summer day.

"Walk with me, Summer," my mother tells me.

We walk down a path; a canopy of magnolia and pecan trees stretches overhead, their lush branches interweaving to form a living tunnel of green. The intoxicating scents of cayenne, curry, and gumbo waft on the breeze, escaping through open windows and cracked screen doors, teasing our senses with promises of culinary delights from nearby kitchens. The afternoon sun pierces through the clouds, and the beams glisten upon our skin. We walk hand in hand with sweaty palms, enjoying each other's company.

"It's not your fault what happened. Stop blaming yourself," my mother says in a soothing voice.

I look up into her hazel eyes, and she smiles reassuringly. My grip tightens on her hand.

"I can only help you so much," she tells me.

"I don't need help, Mommy. I'm okay."

"Marie is much stronger than I am. I can only see you here. I can't enter that other world."

"Mom, what are you talking about?" She looks at me with worried eyes.

"I've said enough. You must figure out the rest."

A cold breeze runs down my arm, and I look around, noticing we're no longer on the walkway by my mother's old shotgun house. We somehow ended up in an old cemetery.

"Do you remember when I used to bring you here?" my mother asks.

I look around, noticing the tall sun-bleached tombstones.

St. Louis Cemetery.

"Yes, I remember."

We walk through a green grassy path, still hand in hand.

"You know my mother used to bring me here as well. She would tell me stories of Marie Laveau and all the miracles she would do. She could heal the sick, conjure spirits, and raise the dead."

I see a single tear running down my mother's wrinkled face.

"Why are you crying?" I ask her.

"Because he's here."

I look around and see no one.

"No one's here," I tell her.

"Charles is here," she says.

Her face begins to morph. No longer am I looking at my mother, but it's as if I'm looking in a mirror.

"You need to wake up," I see and hear myself saying.

I step away.

"Wake up! Now! Wake up! Wake up! You need to wake up before he gets you!" this doppelgänger shouts to me.

RESTRAINED

The bright light from the sun shines in my room and slaps me awake. The call for breakfast echoes in the distance outside my door. Pushing myself up, my body moves inches and then stops. Looking down, white straps cross my body. A soft padded cuff holds my wrists, upper arms, and ankles. A thin, white nylon mesh covers my body from my ankles to my chest.

How am I supposed to pee?

And as the thought comes, so does the urge to pee run down my body and sit on my bladder. Wriggling, twisting, and turning don't budge the nylon mesh. All the air leaves my lungs. My mind can no longer remember to inhale or exhale. An instinct taken for granted.

I can't breathe! I can't breathe!

Inhaling only brings in very little, but I keep trying to inhale and exhale. My heart begins pounding in my chest.

"Help!" I squeeze out my vocal cords, but I'm pretty sure no one can hear my faint cries over the hustle and bustle of those walking and talking on their way to morning breakfast.

Please, God, don't let it end like this, in this place, strapped to this bed.

Wriggling to the left and then the right, each breath becomes harder and harder. My heart pounds in my chest.

I'm having a heart attack. I know it!

The knob to the room twists and turns, then Nurse Rosa slowly walks in carrying a food tray.

"What have you done to get yourself in this?" she asks, shaking her head from side to side. She places the tray on the desk, not even noticing my distress.

"I had a feeling you were going to be trouble, but let me knock on wood because you haven't given me any trouble yet," she says while hitting her hand against the wood desk. She turns to walk back out. Panting for air, I try to speak to her.

"I can't breathe," comes out, barely audible, sweat pouring from my forehead. She stops, turns in my direction, looks at me from head to toe, then runs over to my bedside.

"Help!" she squeezes out her lungs in a tone the entire building probably heard. Moments later, a team of orderlies and nurses take up the room.

"She says she can't breathe."

One nurse shines a bright light in my eyes.

"Get her some oxygen," a tall male nurse yells, and a smaller muscular orderly leaves the room. Out of the corner of my eye, I see Dr. Mocker enter the room and stand by the doorway.

"Rosa, order five milliliters of ten milligram diazepam. Ms. James is having an anxiety attack."

All of the nurses and orderlies exit the room except for Rosa and Dr. Mocker.

"Relax, Summer. Breathe out, now in, out, now in," Dr. Mocker tells me while standing over my bed.

"Go check on the medication I ordered," Dr. Mocker instructs Rosa.

Rosa leaves the room. My chest and stomach rise high with each breath I'm trying to catch. Dr. Mocker sits on the bed. "If I unstrap you, will you try to hurt anyone?" I shake my head from side to side. He begins undoing the cuffs and unlocking the fasteners on the side of the bed. "Just relax, Summer." Dr. Mocker runs his hand up and down my arm slowly and gently. I feel my breath slowly returning. The doorknob twists and the room door opens. The doctor jumps up from his sitting position.

"Here's the diazepam. Would you like me to inject her?" the nurse asks. She then looks at me, then Dr. Mocker. She wrinkles her eyebrows and places the syringe, a bandage, and an alcohol wipe in the doctor's hand. She turns and walks out of the room.

"Bring a wheelchair to take her to my office," Dr. Mocker tells Rosa. Rosa moans a sound and says some words under her breath as she exits the door.

"Summer, this is just something to relax you. You're having an anxiety attack. It will go away shortly. I need to inject this into your arm, okay?" Once again, he strokes me very gently. My body starts to relax.

"Okay," I tell the doctor.

He straightens my arm, wipes the crook with a cold alcohol wipe, then inserts the needle into my vein. I watch as the red solution moves from the needle and into my arm. Looking into the doctor's eyes, I forget what's going on. My breathing becomes eupnea, my heart at peace, and my mind journeys beyond the pain. He takes the needle out and places a bandage over the small hole where a red drop now pokes through.

"How do you feel?"

"I'm feeling better."

"I see your breathing has returned. You just needed to relax."

"Yes, the straps and cuffs made me very nervous."

"If you're up to it, I would like to take you to my office to discuss what happened last night. Are you feeling too drowsy to talk?"

"No, I'm fine." I push my legs off the bed. They hit the cold floor, and I try to stand, but I feel like I've just drunk a tall bottle of tequila. My hands grip the side of the bed to keep from falling."I don't think I can make it."

My legs feel like cooked spaghetti noodles.

"Don't worry. I ordered a wheelchair. Rosa will be back, and she will bring you to my office. I'm heading there now, so I'll see you in a few."

Slowly nodding my head up and down, I don't quite know if I feel like talking, but I do know I don't want to be in this room.

I wait for Dr. Mocker to leave, then slowly get up from the bed and walk to the bathroom, using the wall to help me balance and hold me up. I turn the doorknob and, with gentle ease, pull on the bathroom door. Peeping in, I make sure no one is there before entering. Like a child afraid of Bloody Mary, I quickly turn on the light, slowly walk in, and pull the dirty shower curtain back to make sure no one is hidden behind it. No one's here. I walk over to the toilet and pull down my cotton granny panties, the only type of underwear I have here, and then I sit. The urgency to pee has disappeared, and I just sit. No thoughts or ideas pass through my mind, just relaxation. I feel good. Like floating in the clouds good, a cold glass of lemonade on a hot sunny day good. I could sit here forever.

Suddenly, the light flashes off and then back on. I try to quickly stand but my body moves in slow motion. That medicine really slows down my senses. Pulling my underwear up, with one hand on the wall, I walk toward the door. This room is haunted. Is it Charles trying to communicate with me? Is he after me for killing him? The light flashes off again, but I've already left the bathroom and now stand in the bedroom. I turn, casting a hesitant glance back at the bathroom, the momentary illumination revealing an imposing, shadowy figure. It loomed there, in the doorway, its form stretching to an eerie seven-foot height. The figure bore a dark, human-like silhouette. A light shiver courses through me.

"Leave me alone!" I scream at it.

My eyelids blinked, and in that mere instant, the shadowy presence vanished.

"I'm back," Rosa walks through the door pushing a wheelchair. Relief runs through my arteries and veins.

"Come, have a seat. I'm going to take you to Dr. Mocker's office."

Without saying a word, I have a seat, and she begins pushing me out of the room and down the corridors to Dr. Mocker's office. I don't mention the shadow figure. Would she believe me if I did? What is this apparition I just saw? Is it all in my mind? Was it the medicine the doctor injected me with? I just don't know.

"How are your visits with Dr. Mocker going?" asks Rosa.

"Well, I guess."

"He's a good doctor, especially for the ladies."

Her comment caught me off guard. What exactly does that mean? With so much on my mind, I ride in silence. We pass the cafeteria, and my stomach begins growling. With everything going on, I forgot I didn't eat breakfast.

"Can we go to the cafeteria? I never ate breakfast," I ask Rosa.

"You're not supposed to be in the cafeteria until you're cleared. You're on close watch because of the incident last night. As a matter of fact, you're not supposed to go anywhere throughout here without security, but Dr. Mocker said it is imperative he sees you now, and there wasn't anyone available to escort me with you."

"So, am I supposed to starve?"

"I'll have someone bring your breakfast tray to you."

The rest of the way, she pushes me in silence. As we turn a corner, I can see Dr. Mocker through his open door. He's sitting at his desk, typing away at his computer. With how fast and intense his typing appears, you would think he was writing a novel. We enter his office,

Rosa pushes me until the wheelchair is level with the chair I usually sit in when I'm here, and then she turns and leaves without saying a word.

"Summer, I really wanted us to have this session right away because I want you to tell me everything that occurred last night while it's fresh on your mind."

Dr. Mocker walks over and grabs my hand, gesturing for me to get out of the wheelchair. He walks me over to a plush leather chaise that sits against the wall beside his massive bookcase. I sit on the comfortable chaise and watch as he pulls the chair in front of his desk over and takes a seat.

"Are you comfortable?" he asks.

"Yes."

"The medicine I gave may make you drowsy, so I want to make sure you're in a comfortable position. I would hate to see you fall out of the chair."

"I'm okay. I feel tired but not extremely tired that I would fall over."

"Okay, good. Whenever you're ready, you can begin telling me about last night."

Dr. Mocker sits with an air of profound concentration, his gaze locked onto me as I explain everything that occurred last night. His attentive demeanor suggests he's taking in every word.

"I know this story sounds crazy, but I did not choke her. As a matter of fact, if you watch the security cameras, you'll see that I ran out of the room first, and she came second, knocking me off my feet. I'm not saying she wasn't choked. I'm just saying I didn't do it."

"If you didn't do it, who do you think did it."

"I don't know."

"It definitely happened because she has the marks around her neck to prove it," says Dr. Mocker.

I shake my head from side to side. None of this makes sense. I just don't know what happened.

"Right now, it's your word against hers. We will review the security cameras, but you'll be confined to your room in the meantime."

Quietness circulates the room, and my stomach growling breaks the silence.

"I didn't get to eat breakfast."

"I have some fruit in my bag. Would you like it?"

"Sure."

Dr. Mocker walks behind his desk. He pulls a clear plastic bowl full of fruit out of his bag.

"Here's some mixed fruit I bought at the store."

I pull the plastic lid off and dig in, picking up sliced pineapple with my fingers. He watches me eat. I try to chew it slowly and cutely. I have no idea why I feel so nervous around him.

"Do you eat a lot of fruit?" I ask him.

"I'm on a paleolithic diet. It consists mostly of fruits, veggies, and meat. Some people call it the caveman diet."

"Why are you on a diet?" I laugh as I ask the question.

"I've gained a few pounds over the past few years working here, so I'm trying to get it off."

"You don't look like you need to lose weight to me. You look like you go to the gym every day."

"Actually, I do. I work out six days a week."

"I used to do hot yoga five to six days a week."

"Oh really? My wife was a yoga instructor."

"She doesn't teach anymore?"

"She passed away some months back." Dr. Mocker looks down at the gold wedding band, hugging his finger, and turns it.

"It's hard losing someone you love," I tell him.

He nods his head forward and then looks me in the eyes. His grayish-brown eyes speak to my soul. They warm my spirit and send chills down my flesh. Without even realizing it, my hand covers his large rough hand. Dr. Mocker's gaze leaves me, and he pulls back his hand.

"I'm so sorry. I didn't mean to," I spit out, feeling embarrassed and humiliated. What got into me?

"It's okay," Dr. Mocker tells me as he gets up from his seat, slides it back in front of his desk, then sits in the chair behind his desk.

"Are you okay with sitting over here?"

"Yes, I am." I close the lid on the remainder of the fruit, get up, and slowly walk over to the chair in front of the doctor's desk to have a seat. Dr. Mocker picks up the phone. "Can I have an escort for Ms. James, please?" He puts the phone back on the hook.

"We will be checking the cameras and investigating what happened. Meanwhile, you'll have to remain in your room."

Sitting back in my chair, I put a stray hair behind my ear.

"How long will I be confined to my room?"

My question goes unanswered. We both sit there without any exchange of words. Did I push the boundaries? What was I thinking? Oh wait, I wasn't thinking. This doctor has been so kind to me, and my reaction was to hold his hand. I've lost my husband, and he has lost his wife. I must seem desperate.

"Summer, are you okay?"

"I'm embarrassed. Normally, I don't just grab men's hands like that. I don't know what got into me." My hands rise up to my face, and I cover my eyes.

"Don't feel embarrassed. I'm not judging you. I'm happy you're beginning to open up to me. Before the ECT, you were very standoffish. You would come into my office and just sit there. For days, you watched me type notes and check my emails. I would ask you questions, and you would only stare at me. This is an improvement."

My hands leave my eyes and fall to my lap.

"Can you tell me more about before the ECT? Did I ever mention being afraid to be in my room?"

"You were never afraid to be in your room. This is all new, but I do remember you telling me you and your husband were having problems."

"What type of problems?"

"You have insinuated that he was unfaithful."

"Unfaithful!"

Could I've killed him because he was unfaithful?

"Unfaithful?" I reply again.

We loved each other! Unfaithful, I wonder with who, for how long?

"Did I mention with who or for how long?"

"No, you never gave me much details."

A faint knock comes from the door, and a bald-headed orderly enters the room without waiting for permission.

"Did you call for an escort?"

"Yes, Summer needs to be taken back to her room."

"No problem. Summer, would you like to use this wheelchair?"

"I can walk," I tell the Mr. Clean look-alike while standing to my feet. He walks over to me and puts his hand around my arm.

"I don't need help walking. I feel perfectly fine now." Really, my legs still feel a little noodly, but I want to walk off these drugs.

He lets go, folds the wheelchair, and asks, "Would you like me to return the wheelchair to the nurse's station?"

"Yes, thank you," Dr. Mocker answers. Mr. Clean and I leave Dr. Mocker's office.

Mr. Clean is one of the ones that takes his job seriously. He pulls up in his blue F-150 on time every day. His shirt is always neatly tucked into his starched and creased pants. Some days, he bends down and dusts off his black polished shoes after walking on the gray chalky stones that cover the outside pavement. On other days, he checks his collar to ensure it's neatly bent. He rarely talks to the other workers and never fraternizes with the patients. If I had to guess, he's aiming for a supervisor position.

"Can we stop by the cafeteria?" I ask him.

"No, you have to go straight to your room. I heard about what you did last night, and I'm not taking any chances. We will bring food to your room."

He lifts his shirt a little, letting me see the taser holstered in his belt.

"What do you think I'm going to do? Run? Where would I run? You guys have got us locked in here."

He doesn't respond. He just continues walking beside me at the same slow pace as me.

"How long will they keep me in my room?"

"Dr. Mocker's decision."

"What is the usual timeframe?"

He continues walking with no response.

We approach the nurse's station, and he gives Rosa a half-smile. A security officer walks out of my room as we get near.

"It's clean—no contraband," he tells Mr. Clean.

"Contraband?"

My footsteps into the doorway falter, and a hand touches my back and pushes me the remainder of the way into the room. The door closes, and I hear the lock click.

Was it really necessary for him to push me?

CAGED

Roughing it in this small room has been challenging the past few days. It's always cold and uncomfortable. The food is unpalatable, leaving me wanting to vomit! Communication with the nurses is nearly nonexistent. I can't help but wonder if a touch of hospitality would truly be too much to ask for. How is a person supposed to heal or recover when they are locked up alone and drugged? This is like a real prison, except for the excessive drugs that they push on me. As if they want to make a zombie of me.

Honestly, I've actually been enjoying the drugs; they put me to sleep and help the days pass by. When I awaken, I eat, use the bathroom, and float back into a slumber. I really miss the cafeteria and interacting with Whitney and Eric. I would even talk to Paula right now. I just don't want to be alone.

Thoughts about Charles come and go. I'm trying to remember the last time I was with him, but my mind won't let me think too deeply. It just cruises along the tips of my memories. One undeniable truth remains: we were blissfully happy together. The mere notion of him being unfaithful feels like an unfathomable dream. Our love was profound, an unbreakable bond. Each night, we shared tender kisses before surrendering to slumber. He never hesitated to hold my hand in public, showering it with affectionate kisses. His love for me was evident to anyone in our presence. I remember when I cut my hair short and looked so ugly, he knew how self-conscious I was about my appearance. And without fail, he would remind me of my beauty every single day. Charles had an innate ability to boost my confidence and shower me with affection. It's so hard to believe that I could murder him. I loved him!

TALL DARK SHADOW

Suddenly, my consciousness jolts to life, ripping me from the clutches of sleep. An overwhelming sensation of being watched surges through me, plunging me deep into a pool of fear. With a swift, anxious gesture, I open my eyes, only to find myself in the dimly lit room. My heart sinks as I encounter a tall, shadowy figure, looming like the harbinger of death, casting an eerie gaze upon me. An invisible hand clutches my heart, and my entire body tenses with an electric charge of dread. "I'm here," my racing heartbeat seems to echo, a desperate plea in my chest. Perhaps, I think, if the figure remains unaware of my wakefulness, it might vanish into the shadows. But my clammy hands betray me, trembling beneath the thin veil of the covers. The dark presence slowly pivots, retreating into the bathroom, the door clicking shut behind it. I clutch the covers tighter as if they hold the power to ward off whatever malevolent force lurks in the room. Lost in a surreal trance, I remain motionless, questioning the boundaries between reality and illusion.

Minutes melt into hours, and with each passing moment, the room brightens as the first rays of sunlight pierce through the window, dispelling the lingering darkness. I greet this new day with open arms, grateful for its reassuring light. The lingering unease of doubting my own mind still lingers, a haunting reminder of the night's unsettling events.

Glancing at the clock on the wall, its luminous hands read 6:05 AM, and nature calls—I need to pee. My gaze shifts toward the slightly ajar bathroom door, a gateway into the unknown. I can't help but wonder if anything or anyone might be lurking on the other side. It's funny how the mind plays tricks on us. The boogeyman, a creature of childhood nightmares, doesn't exist in the real world. As for spirits, well, they're not here to cause us harm. At least, that's what I've been told. They can't hurt you; they can only succeed in scaring you, making your own fears come to life. You end up frantically stumbling over unseen obstacles or crashing into things that shouldn't be there. It's all in your head, they say. But in moments like these, the line between reality and imagination blurs, and I can't help but question what might be lurking in the shadows.

What choked the nurse?

Because I didn't.

Was she faking it?

I sit up in bed slowly, rocking back and forth. Could Charles's spirit really be haunting me? What if I really did kill him, and he's now trying to seek revenge on me? Or maybe he's trying to just communicate with me and tell me who did kill him. I squeeze my vaginal muscles together—I really have to pee.

I walk over to my room door and knock on it. It clicks and then opens. Walking over to the nurses' station, I hope my plan works.

"Can I go to the day room to use the bathroom? My toilet has stopped working," I ask Ms. Charlie, the queen on duty. Ms. Charlie was born Charles, but she says she always knew she was supposed to be a woman. She started dressing like a girl in the eighth grade and never looked back. She's one of the slackers here. She's always right on time or a few minutes late. She gets out of her purple Dodge Challenger smoking a skinny cigar with tall heels or clogs and shoes that look like they would be very uncomfortable for this job. I like Ms. Charlie. She has a very eccentric spirit. I can tell she's genuinely a good person on the inside, and most people are not.

"I wasn't even supposed to let you out. I heard about what you did the other night, and you're in trouble, Ms. Thang. You're probably going to be locked in your room for a while," she says.

"I really have to pee."

"You can go, but you have two minutes. Be quick. I don't want to get in trouble. I'll be watching you on the cameras. When you return, I wanna hear all about what happened the other night."

"Cameras?"

"Yes, Ms. Thang, there are cameras back here. Someone is always watching you, so watch what you do."

Once I saw Ms. Charlie on duty, I knew she would let me go. It's a shame many of the other workers don't take her seriously, and some of the patients run all over her. Paula turns her nose up at her every time she sees her, but Paula is mean and rude to everyone. If I'm being honest, I consider Ms. Charlie a friend. I know a lot of people don't understand the LGBT community and may look down on them, but we're who we are, and showing compassion can go a long way; plus, who hasn't experimented with the other side?

Swinging the door to the day room wide open, I'm immediately ambushed by the relentless onslaught of daylight pouring in through the windows. The brilliant luminescence forces my eyes shut instinctively. As I blink them open, a towering shadowy presence looms before me. The strange figure seems to evaporate into thin air as I blink again, leaving me to question my sanity. It's moments like these when I can't help but wonder if I'm losing my grip on reality. Maybe the four walls of this place have finally cracked my psyche. Or perhaps something darker is at play, toying with my perception. Whatever it is, it's unsettling. If they confine me to my room, I won't have the luxury of escaping to the day room whenever fear grips me, especially at night. And let's face it, there's always something eerie about the bathrooms in this place. But the urgency to pee prevails over my trepidation.

The draft from the a/c vents in the bathroom and the day room sends shivers down my spine, and goosebumps rise like an army on my flesh. These days, I'm constantly cold. It's as though my very core has been locked in a sub-zero freezer, chilled to the bone. Cradling myself, I rub my hands up and down my arms in a futile attempt to banish the nagging cold that clings to my skin. I'm learning to adapt to this hell, this twisted existence, to maintain a semblance of sanity. I've got to tell myself that it was all in my head, that there's no way anything could have invaded my room. The shadowy figure was nothing more than fragments of my overactive imagination, right? The nurse's claim of being choked? This is just another twist in this bizarre narrative, perhaps borne out of her personal dislike for me.

I just don't know. My mom always talked about spirits and demons visiting people; tormenting them, making them do things they wouldn't normally do. What if a spirit made me kill Charles? Is it possible I could have been possessed? Is the spirit still haunting me and following me around? But why me?

Walking back to the room, I think about what to tell Ms. Charlie. I know she's going to spread gossip all around this place. Gossip spreads fast in places like this. There will be my version and the version Ms. Charlie fabricates. Then, there will be the versions other people create. I can see Ms. Charlie now, laughing with the other staff, telling them, "She's afraid to go in her bathroom . . . she really is crazy," or, "They were fighting like cats and dogs, and Summer began choking her."

Turning the corner, I see the desk and try to peep at where the cameras sit, but they are very well hidden, and that's if there is even any there at all. Looking out the corner of my eye, I see Ms. Charlie on the phone. Thank goodness, because I really didn't want to talk. She quickly hangs up. "Stop, stop. I want to talk to you." Letting out a breath, I stop and turn toward her. "Ms. Charlie, I'm really not in the mood. My head is hurting, I'm cramping, and I just want to lie down."

"Well, I'm trying to help you. You tell me what happened, and I can put in a good word to the doctor. But if you want to be locked up in your room all week, go ahead, honey. Lie down in your comfy bed. You might as well get used to it."

Exhaling then cracking my tired neck, I sit in the white wicker chair and begin telling her my side of the story, from the time I awoke frightened to now. She listens in awe, looking at me in amazement and making shocked faces with every statement I made. She's so dramatic.

"Ms. Charlie, do you know Whitney?"

"Of course, I know Whitney. I knew her before she even arrived here. My aunt went to her for readings for years. Actually, she had a lot of clients before she came here."

"How did she end up here?"

"I can't give out that information. HIPPA laws and all."

"Can you do me a favor?"

"I don't do favors. I love my job and pay, and I can't risk getting fired, but what 'cha want?"

"Can you please give Whitney a note for me? Please?"

"Okay, but don't tell anyone, I mean anyone. I normally don't do things like this, but there's something about you I like."

Ms. Charlie displays a half-moon smile and slides a piece of paper and pen to me, watching each dotted I and crossed T; she didn't miss a word I wrote on the paper.

For the next two days, my room entertained me with the cracking noises of an old settling house. The sound of the wind sang its best opera, and a hailstorm danced on the cement outside my window. The sound of people walking outside my door has also been entertaining.

I heard Donald, a janitor here, wife is pregnant. He doesn't know how because he says he's sterile.

Jessica, a patient who they call skinny Penny, was caught with contraband in her room.

Delisa, the nurse who was choked, hasn't been back to work since the day of her so-called choking.

These walls are paper-thin, and unless you whisper, someone always hears what's going on.

As for me, I've spent endless hours in this room, my thoughts spiraling. I wrestle with the fragments of memories, trying to piece together the events that led me here and what I can do to get out. Once I do get out, how will I move on with my life? Charles was the breadwinner; how will I support me and my daughter? She has been in private school her entire life and it's not cheap. We were able to wear designer clothes, and I had a lot of designer bags. I miss my bags, Tom Ford lipstick, and Gucci flip-flops; they were my everyday attire. And then there's the unsettling thought that creeps into my consciousness: Charles' insurance policy. Is it wrong to contemplate such material concerns now, amidst the chaos of my existence? What's become of me? Sometimes, the weight of it all bears down on me, and I entertain dark thoughts, those seductive whispers of surrender and escape. It's an unbearable burden, but I can't afford to crumble. I remind myself that there's a life to be lived, a child who depends on me. She's my anchor, my reason to persevere. The malevolent force that seems to pursue me may whisper temptations of an easier way out, but I'll defy it. I'll endure for her sake. And lucky for me, I haven't heard any noises coming from my bathroom or seen any more shadows.

Today, I have an appointment with Dr. Mocker. Hopefully, he will sign off so I can leave my room and visit the day room and the cafeteria again. Lying in bed, the light pierces through from under the door, and the light from the window peeks in, leaving the room dimly lit. Looking at the clock, it's 3:00 AM. I turn on my side and try to fall back to sleep. Breakfast isn't served until nine, and my appointment with Dr. Mocker isn't until eleven.

The room is cloaked in a disconcerting silence until the whining sound of a door opening floats through the room. All I can think of is that damn bathroom door. I cautiously peek through the safety of my covers, surveying the room. To my relief, the bathroom door remains firmly shut. Looking toward the bedroom door, I see it's closed as well. I let out a shaky breath, my racing thoughts finally beginning to ease. I snuggle into the cold embrace of the mattress, and drift off to sleep.

At eleven, a hefty security guard escorts me to Dr. Mocker's office. Apparently, they didn't have a shortage of security today because normally, whoever is at the desk has been escorting me, but today they are actually following protocol. We walk through the vacant halls. No words pass between us, just the sound of our footsteps echoing in the air. We approach the closed door, and the security guard softly knocks. Excitement runs through me; it's lonely being in a room alone. I miss talking to Charles and shooting the shit with my friends, book club meetings, and afternoon lunches at exclusive restaurants. My old life seems like a distant memory, as if I've been reincarnated into hell, but I do feel drawn to the doctor like he's an ally. He seems sensitive to what I'm going through. I'm sure he will get me out of here.

The security guard knocks a little harder.

"Come in," comes from the inside of the door.

The guard barely opens the door. "Hey, Dr. Mocker, I have Summer James here for ya," the guard says with a feminine voice, leaving me shocked. The whole time, I thought the guard was a man. Her shaved head with no make-up, earrings, or any symbol of femininity made me assume she was a he.

"Send her in." The guard steps to the side, allowing me to push open the door and walk in. As I enter, I see Dr. Mocker sitting with his glasses tucked close to his nose.

"Summer, what do you remember about the last time you saw your husband?"

"Um . . . um. No, I don't know."

"You still don't remember?"

Tears flow down my cheeks. Dr. Mocker passes me a box of Kleenex.

"Up until the incident with your husband, there's no other violence on your record." He pauses. "Why, Summer, why did you do it?"

I stand. "I'm ready to go back to my room."

The ally I thought I had is no ally at all. I'm here alone!

"The session has just begun, and we're at the same place we've been since you arrived here." I begin walking to the door. Dr. Mocker appears beside me in seconds.

"I'm trying to help you, " he grabs my hand. It's okay," he softly whispers in my ear. My tears increase. He gently pulls my hand, guiding me to the chaise.

"Summer, I'm going to take care of you."

Maybe he does care.

I sit on the chaise. Dr. Mocker sits right beside me and begins rubbing my shoulder. My head falls against his chest, and the strong masculine scent of his sandalwood cologne enters my nose. Warmth flows through my body. I wish I could bottle this moment and keep it with me in my room. He runs his fingers through my hair.

"Summer, I really want to help you. I don't think you're a bad person, and I don't believe you're capable of the things you have been charged with, but when people are put in difficult situations, they can respond out of character. I want to help you get your memory back so we can move forward and deal with whatever your mind is suppressing," Dr. Mocker says in a caring voice.

I don't respond. I close my eyes, enjoying his touch, smell, and presence. The minute hand on the colossal grandfather's clock that sits in Dr. Mocker's office slowly crept from three to nine. It seems time has slowed, and the only people in the world are just Dr. Mocker and me.

I lift my head off his chest, look into his eyes, and tell him, "I did not choke that lady."

"Okay, that's what's on your mind."

"Tell me again what happened," Dr. Mocker asks me. I tell him about the bathroom door, when we entered the bedroom, and how I ran out. I tell him about the shadow figure I've seen and how I was afraid to go to the bathroom. He listens with a straight, non-judging face.

"I know all this sounds crazy. I really don't know what to make of it myself, but it's really what happened."

"I believe you."

"Dr. Mocker, do you believe in spirits?"

"I believe energy can't be created nor destroyed, just transferred from one form to another. With that being said, I think it's possible for spirits to exist."

"So it's possible I'm not crazy," I say to Dr. Mocker while smiling.

"No, I don't think you're crazy."

"My mother and grandmother believed in spirits. They would try to communicate and get messages from them. My mother told me it runs in our family, but I wasn't into that kind of stuff.

"What were you into?"

"I was into Charles and spending time with him. From the moment I met him, I just wanted to always be in his presence. No marriage is perfect and we had our ups and downs. Arguing over trivia stuff, him not putting the toilet seat down, not picking his clothes up off the floor, not spending enough time with me but isn't all these things normal for couples."

"Do you think he was cheating on you?"

"I can't imagine him cheating on me. He loved me!"

"How would you have reacted if you found out he was cheating on you?'

"I would ki...." Flows from my mouth without thought. I look at the doctor; he looks at me with a straight face, showing no emotion. "I would be distraught," I say softly.

"How do you act when you're upset?"

"It depends on what I'm upset about."

"What's the worst thing you can remember your husband doing and how did you react?"

"In all honesty, I can't remember him ever doing something that just upset me....Well, I did find exchanges between him and a woman on his Instagram. He was asking her for sex. I saw it and didn't even mention it to him. I wanted to gather more information. I think I waited about three to four months before I ever said anything, and when I did, he apologized, and it never happened again. I had access to all his social media accounts. I really didn't overreact or anything. We never ever had any big fights that I can remember. We were really that couple that was in love that everyone envied."

Time seemed to speed up, and the minute hand leaped beside the twelve in a matter of seconds.

"Our session is coming to an end. I'll approve you leaving your room and let them know you're not a threat to anyone. Try to stay out of trouble, and I'll follow up with you in forty-eight hours."

"Thanks, Dr. Mocker," I tell him as I rise from the chaise, wishing I could stay with him in his arms.

"Summer, are you going to be okay in your room?"

I think over everything that has transpired. I don't want to sound crazy, but saying I believe my room is haunted sounds crazy.

"I'll be fine," I lie.

Mr. Clean escorts me to my room in silence. My legs subconsciously make the steps, but my mind runs, searching for answers. Maybe I'm crazy; maybe I've always been crazy, going to a cemetery, praying to someone already dead. Maybe my mom was crazy, and it runs in our genes. She always told me about superstitions; we would pick flowers and take them to Marie Laveau's grave. Some nights, we would pray to her and light candles, but I only did it to make my mother happy. I never really believed.

What if all of that was in vain? Nothing makes sense. I can remember my love for my husband, which was intense. We had been together since we were kids. We were best friends and never kept secrets from one another. Why would I kill him?

"Wait!" Rosa yells from behind the desk.

I stop at the door of my room and walk to her. Mr. Clean right on my heels.

"I can take it from here," Rosa tells him, and he walks off down the hall, pulling his phone out of his pocket and glazing at the screen.

Rosa walks over to a water cooler and fills a cup halfway. She comes back and hands it to me, along with a small cup of pills. Looking down at the pills, I don't want to take them, but Rosa is looking at me right in the face.

"How did your session go?" she asks.

"It went well." As if I would tell her if it went horribly.

"Go ahead, take your meds."

I lift the cup of pills to my mouth, dump them in, then drink the water. Rosa continues to watch me.

"Some of the nurses think you haven't been taking your meds, but I informed Dr. Mocker that I didn't have any problems with you taking your meds. Let's try to keep it that way."

Unconsciously, my eyes roll, and I turn my back to Rosa, walking toward my room. All my life, I have been a Southern charm, always polite and pleasant to everyone, but my charm is disintegrating in this place. My eyes are automatically rolling, and my comments are becoming more and more condescending and rude. It's astonishing how a place can change you into becoming someone you're not.

I sit on my bed and stare at the wall in my room. Not a blank stare but a soul-searching stare that allows me to enter the crevices of my mind, and every time I get to a certain point, I run into fog. Why can't I break through the fog and reach clarity? Something in the corner of my vision gets my attention. A small piece of white paper is lying on the floor by the door of my room.

I collect the paper, unfold it, and read:

Hey Summer,

I'm coming to your room tonight at 1:00 AM.

See you then.

Whitney

She must have received my note. Looking up at the clock, there is so much time between now and one in the morning, and the pills are kicking in. My mind dawdles in and out, a smile appears on my face, and frivolous thoughts jump around. The once-hard twin mattress transforms into an inviting and welcoming place. I lay down, closing my eyes to rest them, but the rest transpires into a deep sleep.

A few hours later, a knock on the room door awakens me. "Dinnertime," says a voice from behind the door. I must have slept right through lunch.

My hair sticks to my face, so I run my fingers through it, trying to fluff it out. The thoughts from earlier still linger in my mind, but a renewed strength sits on my chest and radiates from my stomach. I slip my feet into my shoes, tie them up, and begin my journey to the dining room. It feels good being free again—no more nasty meal deliveries.

Lost in my thoughts, I stroll past the inviting doors of the cafe and find myself standing in front of a janitor's closet, where I hear the sounds of moaning and loud breathing. The door to the room is cracked, and I peek in. I can see a woman bent over, her dress pulled up, resting on her back, and a long slender penis moving in and out from between her pale white thighs. My gaze travels from their entanglement to the man's face, and there, like an unexpected twist in a surreal play, stands Mr. Clean, the woman none other than Paula. The sight strikes me like a surreal vision of savagery. The instinct to flee courses through my veins, and I swivel on my heel to make a hasty exit. But fate, it seems, has other plans. My right foot slips from under me, and I fall. Bracing myself for the fall, I land in the arms of a man. Dr. Mocker, his presence suddenly materializing as if from thin air, holds me securely.

I didn't even realize he was walking toward me. Blood rushes through my body, and crimson floods my cheeks, though I avert my gaze to hide my embarrassment. His concerned inquiry, "Are you okay?" brings a strange mix of comfort and awkwardness. I force a feeble laugh to lighten the mood. "Yes, thanks for catching me," I mutter, casting my eyes downward, reluctant for him to witness my blush. He stands in front of me as if he's waiting for a different answer. I quickly fabricate an excuse, "I was on my way to the cafe for dinner when I passed the doors. I realized it turned around and stumbled into you. I'm so clumsy," I chuckle, a fragile veil concealing my unease.

He takes my chin and lifts it, so I have no choice but to look him in the eyes.

Why is he always touching me?

The pace of my heart speeds up, and all of a sudden, I feel warm all over. His touch really gets to me. It reminds me of when Charles would touch me. I miss getting touched by a man.

"I'm okay," I say to him, not knowing what to say or do.

He looks me in the eyes, and I feel so overwhelmed that I move away and take long strides toward the cafe. I want to get away from him. Although he has been caring and kind to me, I don't want to take his kindness the wrong way.

"Come by my office this evening. I found something in your file that might be helpful to you," he shouts after me, but I don't respond. I continued to walk.

Slowly, I eat my dinner, enjoying every second of being out of the room. The Brunswick bullies look my way, but they don't speak or bother me. I see all the familiar faces except for Whitney and Eric. Once I finish, I take the tray, put it up, and head to Dr. Mocker's office.

LAVENDER

To my surprise, Dr. Mocker has lavender-scented candles burning in his office. I didn't take him for a lavender man. I always think of him as masculine, like the guys in the Old Spice commercials. I guess I would have anticipated the smell of sandalwood or frankincense. But maybe lavender can be considered a manly smell. It seems strange for him to burn candles during a session, but the scent is relaxing and soothing. I actually love the smell of lavender. I would always burn lavender candles in my home and even put lavender essential oils in my tub and take long, hot baths. If only I could relax in the tub here with lavender and Epsom salt. Let me stop thinking about home. I refuse to be sad in front of Dr. Mocker. He looks so handsome today; he has a fresh haircut and shave.

I walk over to the chair I always sit in, in front of his desk. My nerves are jumping under my skin, and sweat is dripping down my underarms. Why are my nerves so on edge? The smell of that candle does something to my insides; my vagina muscles clinch; I want this man. His muscles probes from his button down collared shirt. His gaze seems so intense when he looks at me.

"That candle smells good. Is it lavender?" I ask him, trying to cut through the thick sexual cloud circulating the room, or maybe it's just my mind because my hormones are stirring up a big bowl of stew between my legs. Squeezing my thighs together, my vagina aches as it soaks my panties.

Without a word, he opens his desk drawer and pulls out two glasses and a decanter with brown liquid in it. He pours the liquid into the glasses and slides one of the glasses over to me. The tension in the room consumes me. Is this a test? Is he really going to get me liquor? I grab the glass and smell the contents; the sweet, soothing smell of butterscotch, charred wood, and vanilla enters my nostrils. I close my eyes and inhale before lowering the glass to my lips. I want to savor this movement and experience every second of it. The liquid touches my lips and moves into my mouth, circling my taste buds. The strong, earthy flavor slithers down my throat and burns my chest when I swallow. The muscles in my face draw together, and my eyes squint for a quick second as if I'm sucking a lemon. Dr. Mocker gets the decanter and pours me another. Taking a deep breath, I tilt it to my mouth, hoping the drink will calm my nerves and help me relax. This second round goes down smoother, and my face keeps its composure.

A mist of warm desire moves through me. My nipples become erect. I want him, but does he want me? Is he trustworthy? Does he burn candles for all his patients? Does he pour alcohol for all his patients? Could this be my broken mind abandoning its senses and playing a trickery game on me? Oh, how I want him!

My moist vagina is calling his name. I need this! I need a man in between my legs, grinding against my body, the feeling of sensual pressure gliding in and out of me, stimulating my erotic zones, making my body quiver with exhilaration as I reach epidemic sensations that shiver my being and release streams of organismic pleasure throughout me. More sweat rushes to my underarms. My pussy throbs and its wetness touches my thighs. I sit here, scared of the feelings, the thoughts circulating in my mind, pulsating in my veins. Closing my eyes for a second to try to calm my body, I hear him speak.

"Summer, are you okay?"

I open my eyes, and the truth comes out, "I'm a little nervous." Okay. It was a half-truth. I'm completely and utterly nervous; my body is betraying me, my vagina has begun to think on its own, and it's screaming to me to climb on top of this man, stuff his penis in my vagina, and ride him like a bull as my pussy lips tighten and grip his hard dick.

He gets up from his chair with his glass in his hand and walks over to his bookcase.

"You seem so nervous today," he says as he touches my shoulder. I lose my breath; I can't imagine not doing anything. I want him more than I've ever wanted any man before. Not knowing how to respond, I get up from my chair. He backs up and I walk toward him. As I approach him, the lavender smell fades, and the smell of liquor on his breath moves through my nostrils, dominating the room.

It turns me on more.

I stand in front of him, looking him directly in his brownish-green eyes, his face smooth, caramel, handsome, sexy—I want to devour every inch of him. His stance is tall, hovering over me, and his muscles talking to me; they are telling me he wants me too. The outline of his penis stares at me from his pants. Taking the alcohol glass from his hand, I hold it to my lips and turn it up. It lights more fire under my doubts. They burn and disintegrate. I drop the glass; it falls to the floor and shatters. My lips find his and the minute they touch he pushes me off him.

"What are you doing?" he asks me.

"What are you doing!" I exclaim.

I stand in front of him, looking him dead in the eyes. My hands find the buckle of his pants, and I begin unbuckling them.

"Stop," he whispers but doesn't move my hands. I get down on my knees and continue looking up at him as I undo his belt.

"Summer, stop," he says again, and this time, he grabs my arms and pulls me up. We stare at each other and then his tongue enters my mouth as his hands squeeze my ass. I really don't want the foreplay. My vagina is aching so bad! I want him to enter me now!

I begin undoing his pants, and he slips his hand under my shirt to cup my breast. Before I know it, my shirt is on the ground, and he's kissing and sucking them. The heat in my body elevates, so I pull him by his tie to his desk. He lifts me up, and I wrap my legs around his hard body. His stiff penis pushes against my pants as my heart races and pounds in my chest.

"Fuck me," I hear myself saying.

"Not yet," he whispers in my ear.

I want to explode as he lays me on the desk and begins pulling off my pants. He leaves my panties on but starts kissing and touching my vagina through them.

"Please fuck me," I say as he tears my wet panties off and puts his finger in me. He takes it out and puts it in his mouth, then fingers me again and sticks his fingers in my mouth.

"You taste sweet, don't you," he says while he kisses the crevices between my legs and vagina, and then his mouth moves to my labia, then back up to my stomach. He licks around my nipples and keeps moving up to my mouth.

Once again, I feel his penis against my vagina, but this time, there's nothing in between, flesh to flesh. The smoothness of his manhood rubs up and down the lips of my vagina, entering the crevice a tidbit before pulling back out, driving me insane. He reaches down and circles the inside of my kitty just enough to make me want to scream. I ache for him to enter me fully.

He puts the tip in, then pulls it out. A tear rolls down my face—this is torture in the worst way. He keeps moving his penis up against my vagina. It feels good, but I need him to enter my wet pussy, and then he does. I exhale, sheer pleasure overcoming my body. His penis is long and thick, and he takes his time, moving in and out of me, my vagina pulsating more and more, gripping his big hard dick. Oh my God, I never felt this way before; ripples of pleasure run all over my body, my pussy pulsating so hard.

"Dr Mocker!" I scream, and he begins pounding my pussy, harder and harder, his muscles rubbing up against my breast; sweat from his forehead glides down my face, and before I know it, I have the best orgasm I have ever had.

He continues in me until he finally comes. He slowly pulls his penis out of me and starts to kiss my breasts. Shivers run up and down my body. For so long, I had yearned for something sexual. He moves off me, and then we both begin to dress; the smell of pleasure lingers in the air.

He kisses me on my cheek and whispers, "See you at our next session."

I leave his office, trying to walk straight and look normal. I approach my room door, turn the knob, and there, lying in my bed, is me, sleeping. I stare at myself, my black hair braided back. My caramel skin, my wrinkled face, the darkness around my eyes. The sadness my face portrays as I sleep. My heart drops to my feet. I try to pick it up, but it's like lifting a 100-pound weight. I leave it there on the floor and walk over to myself. I begin to stroke my face—I pity myself. Then, I awaken. It was just a dream, a vivid dream at that. How could my mind betray me like this?

REVELATION

One A.M. comes with the slowness of an inchworm. I sit on the edge of my bed, leg shaking, palms sweaty, waiting for Whitney to come to my door. 1:01, and she's still not here. Can time speed up? My nerves can't take the anticipation any longer. Standing to my feet, I pace the floor. 1:02. What if she doesn't come? What if the note is from someone pretending to be her? How is she even going to get out of her room at this time?

Picking up the letter, I read her small cursive writing. Maybe she fell asleep. I walk over to my small window of entertainment; a beautiful, glowing full moon rests in the sky, and a few stars stare back at me. A streetlight reveals the quiet parking lot where very few cars sit. Not many people work at night. A plump security guard leans against the rail of the stairs leading to the door of the building. He lights a cigarette. He's probably going to be there for a while. Only two security guards work at night, and both are slackers. They punch in and out. Their main concern is their paycheck. The sound of footsteps gathers at my door.

I look at the clock—1:04.

The doorknob twists, and Whitney walks in. Relief rolls over my body. Happiness overcomes me, and before I know it, I'm hugging the pure lady like a long-lost friend I just found.

"Well, hey there, Summer."

"I'm happy to see you. I have so many questions, and I'm so confused, and something in me tells me you can help me." I exhale, then begin again: "First off, how are you able to get out of your room?"

"I got friends in high places," she says with a smile.

"I didn't see you in the cafeteria today."

"Sometimes, I like to sit in my room and eat. I can feel people's energy; sometimes, it becomes overwhelming, and I need a break from people. Do you mind if I take a seat on your bed?" Whitney asks as she walks to the bed.

"Sure."

Whitney takes a seat and beckons for me to sit beside her.

"Your note said you want me to do a reading on you," Whitney stated.

"Yes. I need to know if I killed my husband—it doesn't seem right. I loved him with every inch of my core."

Her gray eyes penetrate mine, and her expression shows she can see right through my soul. Her smile dissipates, and she begins looking at me with a stern face and says, "Are you sure you want to know what happened?"

"I'm one hundred percent positive!"

She grabs my hand. "I will show you, but there's no turning back after this."

Whitney's hands cuff mine. Her palms feel warm and comforting but sweaty.

"Just relax and calm your mind," she whispers in the silent room.

I look at the clock, 1:15. Now, 1:20 comes, and we're still sitting in silence. Should I say something? My mom used to give readings, which went a lot differently than this. She would read palms or use tarot cards. She said Marie guided her readings. I had always wished I had the gift and sometimes felt like I did, but I never knew anyone's future or past. Once, my mom even went to Marie's grave, lit candles, and prayed for hours for me to have the gift, but I never received any powers or gifts. I'm just plain ole Summer, who murdered her husband, I guess.

"Calm your mind," Whitney whispers again.

This seems like total bull crap. There are so many fake people who claim they have the gift. Truth be told, only a few people really have it.

"I see glimpses of you with a young child, a girl between the ages of five and seven. She has short, brownish-curly hair. Her skin is a watery caramel complexion. Do you recognize this image?"

I nod.

"That's my daughter, Angelique," I whisper.

This is the first time I have said my daughter's name since I've been here. Her name feels sharp, coming from my mouth. It's been heavy on me, like a pile of bricks on my shoulders, and when I spoke it, my heart skipped a few beats. My breathing stops for a few seconds. Whitney interrupts my pain. She drops my hands, touches my heart with her left hand, and touches my forehead with her right.

She begins a quiet chat, "Take her back, merciful angel. Show her the pain." Over and over, she says the words, and they take over my mind, rolling along my thoughts, moving in me like a song, and I want to dance to their rhythm. The air becomes thin, the temperature drops even lower, and before me appears a large white light in the shape of a woman. She stares at me with a beautiful, caring smile. She puts her hand over her heart as a sign of love and then drops it back to her side. The warmth of her gesture encompasses me.

It's Marie!

My breath leaves my body. Gasping for air, I fall back.

Quickly, I sit up and begin to frantically look around. Whitney is gone. The room's color is a light gray with a darker gray accent wall. The linoleum floors are replaced with cream of wheat Berber carpet. Next to me stands a tall mahogany bed with a beautiful white canopy. I'm home. I inhale and exhale with excitement. My legs begin to shake as I stand up. Overwhelming disbelief circulates in me.

"I'm home! I'm home!" I cry out, and then that cry turns into a different cry. A cry of anger. Laying upon my white sheets is an abomination. My body grows hot with pure hatred and fury. My hands soak with sweat, and involuntary warm tears accumulate and circle my eyes until two trails of hurt roll down the sides of my enraged face. The smell of sex and sweat waves in the air and enters my nostrils. Before I know it, I'm yanking at the sheets, but it doesn't cause any disturbance.

"How could you, after all these years?" I yell at my husband as I lunge at the woman moving on top of him. Her body grinding on my husband's penis.

My goal is to grip her and sling her off my husband. Instead, I fall through her and land on the floor. Getting up, I use every grain of strength in me to grab the woman and throw her off my husband, but once again, I fall right through them, landing on the floor. I place my hands across from my eyes, wondering what is going wrong, and then it hits me: I'm only here in spirit. This is a memory.

A faint knock echoed through the room's silence. The sound escaped everyone's notice except mine. Once again, a gentle tap on the door, and as it opens, there stands Angelique. My heart swells, my baby! My baby! Oh, how I missed her; sadness stirs at the pit of my core; every cell in my body wants to embrace her and never let go. Tell her I've missed her and don't ever want to be separated again; let her know I'm here and will always be here for her. This is my baby! I want to plant tons of kisses upon her and just hold her till day turns to night and recycles once more, but as I approach her, a grim realization crashes upon me. I can't hold her. I'm only here in spirit. I follow her gaze and at this moment, she's witnessing her father and this whore. She can't see her father with this woman. The image will be stamped in her mind forever. In desperation, I put my hands over her eyes as I plead with God for her not to see through them. How many times can my heart explode before the pain overcomes all my thoughts, and I surrender to my sinister thoughts and let Satan take over my body and do as he pleases? One person can only take so much. I guess this is why I murdered him. And then, I see my actual, physical self run into the room and grab Angelique. My husband looks up and pushes the woman off him. That's when I realize who she is.

Christina Mocker.

My husband's secretary.

Mocker!

"Go to your room," I hear myself yell at Angelique. I watch as I grab Christina by her streaked blonde hair. I begin to try to drag her out of the room. My eyes don't even dart my husband's way until I see him walk over and slap me across my face.

"She's with child," he screams at me, his French accent materializing.

A door slams, my eyes begin rapidly blinking, and that's when I realize I'm back in the dreary hospital room, no Charles, no Christina, no Angelique.

"You ladies need to wrap it up. Whitney, you got to get back to your room. I can get in a lot of trouble for this," Ms. Charlie says as she peers at us.

Whitney rubs her hand down my shoulder. "Are you okay, hun?" My thoughts collide and bounce against the walls of my mind. Rage boils in my blood and warms the vessels in my heart.

He had cheated, she was pregnant, I was pissed, and I killed him?

Sitting still on the bed, I watch Whitney get up and walk over to the door. "Are you going to be okay?" she asks.

With my mouth arrested, I stare at the wall.

"She'll be okay," says Ms. Charlie.

They leave the room, and my body falls back against the mattress.

CHRISTINA MOCKER

Rays from the sun shine into my room. The darkness races to oblivion. I continue to lay in my bed, staring up at the peeling popcorn ceiling. A headache sets in from not sleeping and from using every cell in my body to wrap my mind around what happened in my home that night. What did it lead to?

Most importantly, who is Christina Mocker?

It seems his betrayal drove me overboard and made me kill him, but I'm not a violent person. Growing up, I never got into any fights. Rarely even had any verbal altercations with anyone. I can't fathom killing someone. I know I was utterly and intensely upset, but I don't think I could commit murder. I can't imagine stabbing someone to death; that's brutal. How long was he cheating?

I still haven't received my phone call, and I don't even know who has custody of my daughter. Darlene, they said. But who knows? She's her godmother. She has always been a good aunt to Angelique and she loves her. I do know I can trust her. But I really need some family right now. My mom is gone, and I've been estranged from my family for years because of Charles. Charles was my go-to for everything. Now that I think about it, he controlled my life. He told me how to dress, how to wear my hair, and where I could work. He even told me who and who not to be friends with. I was so consumed with him and what he wanted. He received all of me and still cheated.

Last night's biggest revelation is Christina Mocker, his secretary and wife of Dr. Mocker. When I saw his picture in the corridor, I knew I had seen it somewhere, and now I remember. A picture of him and Christina sat on her desk. Her desk was located right beside Charles' office, and every time I went in, I would always look at the picture and think, "What a beautiful couple."

Last night, after Whitney left, I was punched in the face with so many memories but no memories of killing Charles. I remember going to his office, talking, and laughing with Christina. I never suspected she would cheat with Charles. I loved Charles, but he was plain. A handsome man with the gift of the gab, but he didn't dress extravagantly. He didn't drive a flashy car or have a doctor's degree like Dr. Mocker. He always went to work and came straight home. He was mine. I never felt I had to worry about him cheating.

Christina is a diva. She always wears the latest fashion and the most expensive brands. She drives the newest model Mercedes sports car. She would come into the office with her gold and diamond earrings and Cartier watch, but I guess you can do that when your husband is the Chief physician in a psychiatric hospital. Everyone in the office knew she was married to a doctor. She couldn't wait for the opportunity to bring it up in conversation.

"My husband is a doctor, and I really don't have to work, but I enjoy it. I like having something to do." Or her all-time thing to say was, "This job keeps me from spending all my husband's money, ha-ha-ha." Although, normally, she would be the only one laughing.

She pretended to be so happy in her marriage. I never in a million years thought she would be a threat to mine. In addition, she and I are complete opposites; my everyday attire consists of yoga pants, T-shirts, and tennis shoes. I'm the 'hang with the fellows, tomboy' type, and she's the girly girl. She would wear low-cut shirts and tight pants—the same clothes Charles would make me change out of if I dared try to wear them, but I guess maybe he started to try something different.

Charles said she was with her child. Is it his child or Dr. Mocker's? He reacted as if it was his child. He made me tie my tubes a year ago. He told me he didn't want any more children, and since he didn't like using protection, he thought it would be best for me to tie my tubes. It was a hurtful decision because I always envisioned a big family, but I loved Charles, and that's what he wanted, so that's what I did.

What puzzles me the most is why Dr. Mocker said his wife was dead. Did he know they were having an affair? Does he know I caught them? I've got to find out how much he knows and if his wife really is dead, and if so, what happened to her?

The sound of many footsteps approaches from under my door. I know it's breakfast time, but I'm really not in a breakfast-type of mood. Ms. Charlie told me it's best to never skip a meal because the staff becomes suspicious—they think something is wrong and make documentation of it in your file. She says it's best to act as normal as you possibly can act in a place like this. So, I guess it's best for me to pull myself together and shower yesterday's remnants and this morning's new anxiety away.

In the cafeteria, I see Whitney and Eric sitting together. I grab a yogurt and an apple and walk over.

"Hey, hun, how are you this morning? You didn't sleep much, did cha?" Whitney asks as I approach them. I guess sleep deprivation is written all over my face.

"After my session with you, so many memories started to return."

"That's good, hun," she says as she shoves a piece of French toast in her mouth.

"Soooo, do you remember what happened?" Eric asks.

I know he's asking about the night I supposedly killed my husband. "That night hasn't come back."

We sit there quietly, everyone eating for the next few minutes. I see Dr. Mocker walk in and sit with some other staff members.

"Is it true that Dr. Mocker's wife is dead?" I ask Eric and Whitney. Eric drops his spoon in his fruity-looking cereal and looks over at Dr. Mocker, then at me.

"From what I hear, she died in a fire some months back," he says as he looks back down at the cereal and pushes the bowl away.

Whitney remains quiet, snacking on her French toast and stuffing long, thick bacon slices into her mouth.

"No one really knows much about Dr. Mocker. He rarely has patients, and when he does they are all female. I rarely even see him talking to the staff members unless he's giving instructions. Still, I would love to be a fly on the wall in his office because I think something is off with him. Why do you ask about his wife?" asks Eric.

It circles my mind whether I should mention Dr. Mocker's wife and the affair, but I really don't know Whitney or Eric. If Whitney's a good psychic, she should already know. Discussing it will probably only cause rumors to circle the halls, and the less I say, probably the better.

"Just curious because he still wears a wedding ring and mentioned her being dead, so I was just curious," I tell them.

"Oh wow, he's telling you personal information," says Eric.

"Well, he didn't go into detail, and I thought it would be rude to ask questions."

Eric starts back up, eating his cereal. Whitney puts the last piece of French toast in her mouth and says, "Hun, be patient. Your memory will come back—Marie told me."

"I think I saw Marie last night when you were with me. A bright figure appeared that resembled her," I tell Whitney.

"Oh my, she revealed herself to you? She doesn't reveal herself to just anybody. Like I told you before, there's something special about you."

"When did you realize you were psychic?" I ask Whitney.

"I'm not a psychic. Please don't ever refer to me as one," says Whitney as she rolls her eyes at me.

"I'm so sorry. I didn't mean to offend you. My momma was psychic, and that's how she put a roof over my head growing up."

"It's okay. I just really don't like that term. My momma told me I was born with a veil over my eyes. Ever since I was a small child, I could see people that had passed away. Their spirits would talk to me and tell me things. I don't know anyone's past or future. Still, I can communicate with the spirit world, and they relay messages to me and tell me things about people. For example, sometimes, when I see you, I can see a bright glow of light following you, and that bright glow is Marie. You musta did something really special to have her watching over you."

"I remember being at her tomb that night, and I remember putting the X's on it but that's all I can remember about that night," my voice trails off.

"I guess the x's" worked, Whitney says under her breath.

Eric scrunches up his face revealing he has no idea what we are talking about.

"Marie comes to you when you put x's on her tomb and she's supposed to grant your wish." I tell her.

"So, what was your wish," he asks me.

"Your guess is as good as mine, I remember being there, the tall green grass, the tomb, people standing around arguing but then it all fades."

"Can you see my husband, Charles?" I ask Whitney.

"No, I can't. He would have to reveal himself, and he has not."

"I know I'm asking a lot of questions, and I apologize for my ignorance, but my mother never shared much with me, only silly superstitions and tales of Marie. If you don't mind, can you tell me how you were able to help me remember last night?"

She sits down her glass of orange juice and tells me. "I was only following Marie. She told me to touch you and chant, and that's what I did, nothing more. I'm sorry, Summer, but I must return to my room. I'm feeling lightheaded. I'm happy I was able to help you last night."

Whitney gets up, takes her tray, and leaves the table. Eric looks at me with a smirk.

"Guess what?" he says.

Before I can answer, he begins, "I found out why Whitney is in here."

"Okay." My interest in Whitney has left; I'm too caught up in my own issues to really care.

Eric doesn't seem to notice the 'I don't give a damn' expression on my face, and he starts running his mouth, "She was giving a reading to some lady, and afterward, the lady went home and hanged herself. The lady's family was trying to sue Whitney and get the police to arrest Whitney because they claimed they found a suicide letter that said Whitney told her to hang herself.

"They eventually arrested Whitney and got her to take a plea deal for a mental evaluation and a two-year stay here. I've heard that she has been here for over three years. Every time it's time for her evaluation to get out, she does something crazy. It's like she doesn't want to leave. The last time her evaluation came up, she left her room like she was going to breakfast, took off all her clothes, and started dancing in front of the camera. When the guard came, she picked up one of these wicker chairs that sat in the hall and hit him with it. I just can't wrap my mind around it. Who wants to be in here? It's like being in jail," says Eric.

"It's nothing like being in jail. Most of us have our own rooms, and we have the freedom to leave by ourselves during the daytime. We can't leave this floor because of the locked doors, but we have the option of being in our room or the dayroom and going to the cafeteria. Jail is a harsh place, and I would never compare this place to jail. My brother did time, and I would visit him, and the stories he gave were horror movies compared to this. And I must add, the food is not too bad here—we have choices. There are no food options in jail."

Eric looks at me with his eyebrows crinkled, then lets out a laugh. "I guess the food isn't too bad," he says.

Before I can catch the words from coming out of my mouth, I ask Eric, "So, why are you in here?"

I hope he doesn't feel like I'm prying, but he's so quick to talk about Whitney.

He looks around the room, takes a deep breath, then drinks a sip of water. I wait, looking at him in his bright green eyes for an answer. The smirk he had before has transformed, and now his mouth is twisted, and he has a look of disgust on his face. He places his plastic cup on the table and runs his fingers through his blond hair. The seconds pass in slow motion as I wait for a response. The funny thing is, if we were outside this place, Eric and I would have never shared a conversation. He's a preppy, frat kid in his early twenties who probably still lives with his parents and has access to Daddy's money. We have absolutely nothing in common but our imprisonment here.

"Where should I begin?" Eric starts in a whisper as if he's telling me a spooky bedtime story.

"I had been partying with some of my friends down on Bourbon Street during Mardi Gras, and on my way home to Baton Rouge, I was in a car accident. They ruled the car accident my fault because I was way over the limit for alcohol when they gave me a breathalyzer test. I need more water. I'll be back."

Eric gets up and starts walking over to the beverage station. So he's in here for drunk driving. I've never heard of that before. I open my yogurt, lick the foil, and begin eating. I look over and see Brunswick Bullies sitting at a table together, laughing like someone just said the funniest joke ever. Eric approaches and sits back down.

"So, they've got you in here for drunk driving?" spills out my mouth.

He looks at me for a few seconds. "Not exactly," he says and takes some sips of water.

"Someone died in the accident, and the sons of bitches tried to charge me with murder, but my dad wasn't having it. My dad has been a lawyer for over thirty years. He knows all the prosecutors and judges. His best friend is the governor. It was Mardi Gras, for God's sake. Everyone on the streets had been drinking."

I didn't quite know how to reply to that statement. He seems more upset that they tried to charge him than that he had killed someone.

"I was able to come here instead of getting a manslaughter charge. They told my dad there had to be some kind of repercussions. My dad talked to the prosecutors about how I've been dealing with depression ever since my mom passed, and they arranged a plea for me to come here," Eric says, then finishes his water.

Unsure how to open the doors of conversation again, I just sit there, playing with my yogurt and pretending to eat it.

"Everyone here has a story. The prosecutor sometimes tries to put people here who have committed crimes when he doesn't have solid evidence, so he will trick them into taking a plea to come here instead of going to trial and risking jail time. Most people would rather sign off to come here than spend time in jail, but that's only when there's room in here," says Eric.

"Is that even legal?"

"Yes, absolutely. Especially if the person has dealt with mental illness in the past."

"You sure do know a lot," I tell him.

"The privilege of being the son of a lawyer. My dad keeps me informed," he says with a laugh.

My mind begins to drift—I wonder if they didn't have much evidence on me, and that's how I ended up here, and if they didn't have much evidence, maybe it wasn't me that did it.

"Are you okay?" Eric asks.

I've been so consumed in my thoughts that I forgot I was sitting with someone.

"I'm fine. Just wondering how much actual evidence they had on me."

"Maybe you should discuss that with Dr. Mocker. Maybe he can help," Eric says as he rises from the table.

"I'll catch you later, Summer."

"Bye, Eric."

I decide not to linger in the cafeteria by myself. I don't want any more run-ins with the Bullies, so I deposit my tray and head back to my room to contemplate all this new information.

My husband was cheating with Dr. Mocker's wife, Dr. Mocker's wife died in a fire, Whitney communicates with spirits, and handsome Eric, who I thought was sweet, seems a little heartless. He killed someone and has no remorse! All of this seems like a Lifetime movie!

A HELL OF
A NIGHT

The day rolls out, and night comes so briskly. The hard mattress against my body wrestles with my muscles. My shoulders and neck scream for release as if they are toting mountains of cement and bricks. I stretch my neck to the left and then the right, and the sounds of bones cracking vibrate out my skin. Two bricks lift, but there's still more mountain to climb.

Cloudy thoughts swim through the dark channels of my mind, backstroking through wishes, trying to reach the faded memories lying in my subconscious mind. Coldness from the loud air conditioner blows down my paper-thin sheets, soaking the threads and sending chills all over my body. The whistling sounds of the wind play at my window. Dark gray pregnant clouds move across the dimming sky. Pressure builds in my bladder, but I just lie here. Too lost in the vaults of my mind to concentrate on one little urge.

"Why cheat with Charles?" keeps playing in my mind like a broken record. Low voices seep under my door from the hallway. The sounds of the nurses changing shifts. I turn away from the door, close my eyes, and try to clear my mind and focus on falling asleep.

"One sheep, two sheep, three sheep, four—" Off I drift to the Sandman's lair.

Vibrations stir my sleep. I awaken to the bed, moving from left to right. Sitting up, I look around me, but no one is there. "Help," I consistently scream at the top of my lungs. The bed continues to move, and then it begins moving up and down toward the ceiling. I move to the side to try and jump out, but it's like a force field is around the bed. The smell of smoke enters my nostrils. I gasp and cough, swirls of grayish-white fog circulate over my head, and I start suffocating on the fumes. The door to the room opens, and Ms. Charlie walks in and cuts the light on. The room fills with light, the fog disappears, and the bed drops to the ground.

"What in the hell was that?" Ms. Charlie yells. Patting, trying to catch my breath, I have no explanation. She walks over and begins examining the bed.

"You got some weird shit going on with you. I'm going to get out of here because I don't want to get choked. Meet me in the hallway."

Still in complete shock and fear, I just sit on the bed, trying to figure out what just happened, my mind in shambles, thoughts speeding in the HOV lane.

In the hallway, I see Ms. Charlie standing at the nurse's desk, her phone to her ear and a pack of cigarettes in her shaking hand.

"I need a smoke. I'm sweating like a whore in a church house. You got my nerves jumping out of my skin. One of the security guards is coming to relieve me for a few minutes," she tells me as I approach.

"Can you explain to me what was going on in there?" Ms. Charlie asks.

I look into his frightened eyes and shake my head no.

"I've heard of some crazy shit, but I've never seen no shit like that in my life." Exhaling a gigantic breath, I tell him, "I think my dead husband is haunting me."

"Your dead husband? Baby, this is too much for me."

A tall, thin security guard walks up.

"You called for a break, right?"

"Honey, you have no idea," Ms. Charlie says as he walks off. The guard looks down at his watch.

"Shouldn't you be asleep?"

I try thinking of what to say. If I say I just woke up to my bed shaking and lifting off the ground, he will only think I'm crazy. He stares at me, waiting for an answer.

"Why are you not in your room asleep?"

"Oh, I'm sorry. I didn't quite hear you the first time. I couldn't sleep, so I came out to talk to Ms. Charlie."

"Well, she's on break now, so you must go to your room."

"Okay."

I look at my room door, and my body heats. I begin to realize my breath is missing—I'm gasping for air, and my heart leaps repeatedly. Telling myself in, out, in, out, I try breathing, but there is no air to inhale or exhale. I begin feeling lightheaded, and my heart runs a marathon in my chest. Before I know it, I'm falling to the ground. Everything in my visual is spinning. I hear the sounds of the security guard's shoes coming toward me and his voice asking, "Are you okay?" The bright overhead halogen lights seem as bright as the sun at midday, and my head pounds. With blurred vision, I see him pick up his walkie. My eyes close, but I hear everything.

"Jean, what's your twenty?" says the guard.

A voice comes back, "I'm talking a leak."

"Find Ms. Charlie and have him come back to his station immediately. One of the patients passed out."

"Ten-four."

The guard kneels down and props my head on his knee. I open my eyes.

"It's going to be okay. Someone is coming. Can you tell me what happened?" the guard asks me. Shaking my head, my body feels weak and drained of energy, and my breathing is very shallow.

"Can you stand?"

"I think I can." My voice is low and weak. He helps me off the ground and guides me over to the wicker chairs. I sit down, and breathing begins to get easier and easier.

"Is everything okay?" Ms. Charlie asks as she approaches us.

"Right after you left, she fell."

"Summer, you okay?" Ms. Charlie asks.

"I'm having trouble breathing. I was walking to my room and lost my breath."

"I think you're having an anxiety attack. I see in your file you're prone to them. Dr. Mocker authorized medicine for it in case it happens after hours. I'm going to get it. Two doors down is an empty room. How about you sleep there tonight?"

"Okay. Thank you," I tell Ms. Charlie.

"So, is everything okay here? Can I leave?" the security guard asks.

"Go ahead. I got this under control," Ms. Charlie tells the guard as she waves him off.

My head is still spinning, my heart is racing but at a slower pace. I'm scared, with so many emotions rumbling through my veins. Ms. Charlie escorts me to the room. The room is very much similar to the room I occupy. Same furniture, same bed, but a bigger window. I lay down.

"I'll be back in a few minutes with the medicine," Ms. Charlie tells me.

"Is there anything I can get you?

"A blanket," I whisper.

"Of course. I'll bring one back."

The door creaks as Ms. Charlie exits the room.

What a hell of a night.

Either this place is definitely haunted or Charles is trying to get me back for killing him, and if I killed him, maybe I deserve this! Regardless if he was cheating, he didn't deserve to die. Perhaps we could have gotten counseling and worked through it or, worst case scenario, got a divorce. If the child was his, I could have accepted it and helped raise it, but his death should not have been an option. I remember when we were dating and he looked me in my eyes and told me, "I'll never cheat on you or disrespect you, I only want to protect you and take care of you, speak life into you, and do anything I can for you. I wanna give you the world." His statements melted my heart and I believed every word he spoke. He must have really put me in a bad situation for me to even fathom murdering him. I loved that man!

The door creaks again, and Ms. Charlie walks back into the room. She hands me two pills and a small plastic cup of water. Then she takes a thick, beige blanket from under her arm and places it on the bed.

"You guys have blankets this thick? I've been freezing under these sheets!"

"Did you ever ask for a blanket?"

"No."

Ms. Charlie shrugs her shoulders.

"I want to see you swallow these pills," she tells me.

I swallow the pills, open my mouth, and move my tongue to let her know they are gone.

"Now lay down and try to relax. I'm going to prop your door open just in case you need me," she says as she turns her back to walk out of the room. I lay down in the bed on the hard mattress; at least now I have the blanket to keep me warm, and the big window showers the room with streams of dim light.

Tomorrow, I will talk to Dr. Mocker and find out how much information he knows. Hopefully, he doesn't hold back. How could Charlene cheat on Dr. Mocker? He's so handsome and gives her everything she could want. If he was my husband, I would never have cheated on him. I would be a good wife. We should at least sleep together since our spouses did. Wait that's a crazy thought, but that dream I had about him was so good and pleasurable.

If only . . . Maybe we could . . .

Fuzzy thoughts travel in my mind as I try to stay awake, but whatever Ms. Charlie gave me adds pounds to my eyelids, and I just can't hold them open. Sleepiness sets sail, and my mind drifts away. Hopefully, it will be a peaceful night.

BREAKFAST

Footsteps awaken me, and a cold chill flows over me. The two thin sheets covering me do no justice, and the warm blanket Ms. Charlie brought me sits on the floor. Looking over at the door, it's shut, but the morning light brightens the room. I try to sit up, but my limbs feel flaccid, and my mind is crowded with fog. Vaguely, I remember last night, and I search my mind for what exactly happened. The bed shook somehow, Ms. Charlie came in, we both ran out, maybe . . . and I think I fainted or had an anxiety attack. Rubbing my temples, I try to bring forth clarity. Each thought slowly floats, like clouds in the sky, sitting for a moment and then slowly sailing away.

Someone knocks on the door and then opens it. It's Rosa.

"Good morning, Summer. Will you be going to breakfast this morning?" she says with a smile. In my first encounter with her, she was rude, but ever since then, she's been nice, and I've grown quite fond of her.

"I feel exhausted."

"According to the notes, you had a long night. I can bring you a tray of food or push you over to the cafeteria if you like."

"I think I would prefer the cafeteria."

"Okey dokey. Get dressed, and I'll be back in about ten minutes with a wheelchair."

"Thank you!"

Rosa leaves the room, and I wrestle with the sluggishness running through my body. I decided to skip a shower because I would hate falling in the bathroom. Putting on clean clothes, my body moves with the slowness of a tortoise. Sitting in the chair by the desk, I slip my tennis shoes on and feel dizzy as I attempt to tie them. Each motion is so complex and cruel to perform. Rosa opens the door and comes in, pushing a wheelchair. Getting up from my seat, I try to walk over to it but have to stand still and steady myself for a few moments between steps.

"Let me help you," Rosa says, walking over and grabbing my arm. "Are you sure you don't want to eat in here?"

"I would really like to be among other people," I tell her.

"Whatever you want, my dear."

She helps me into the chair, puts my feet up, and finishes tying my shoes. I really like Rosa. As she pushes me to the cafeteria, it seems as if we're moving too fast, and the speed turns my stomach and makes me feel nauseated. I close my eyes and put my head down. I don't even realize when we arrive. Rosa hands me a tray and takes me along the buffet, adding the foods I tell her to add. She then pushes me over to a table.

"What would you like to drink?" she asks me.

"Cranberry juice, please."

She walks away. Looking up, I see Eric sitting at a table by himself. He picks his tray up and walks over to me.

"You must have done something bad," he says as he sits his tray in front of me and sits. Looking at Eric, his words run through my thoughts, and although I comprehend him, I don't quite know how to answer him.

"What?" I choke out.

"I'm sorry, Summer."

"What do you mean you're sorry?"

"I hate to see you in this situation. Do you have any family to check on you?"

"In what situation?" I feel so lost trying to communicate with Eric. I don't understand what I missed or what he's saying or, in all honesty, if I'm floating in a dream.

"They really take advantage of some people, and I've been wanting to say something, but I keep quiet because I want to make sure that when it's my time to go home, I don't have any problems. My dad told me to keep my head down, talk to a few people, and do my time. In addition to telling them whatever I think they might want to hear. But something draws me to you. It's weird."

"Take advantage" plays in my mind. Take advantage how? Eric reaches over and rubs my arm.

"You'll be okay," he whispers.

Rosa walks up and puts the cranberry juice on the table.

"I'll be back in about fifteen minutes to get you," she says, then turns and walks to the cafeteria door. Eric watches her exit.

"I don't know why she brought you here like this?"

"I wanted to eat in here," slowly flows from my lips.

I look down at my eggs and bacon. They don't look appealing, and I can't imagine putting them into my body. I get the cranberry juice and take sips from it.

"Am I dreaming?" I ask Eric.

Eric looks at me and shakes his head. His lips turn up, and a frown appears on his face.

"You're not dreaming, but whatever they gave you, I wish I had access to it on the streets. My friends and I would have had a good ole' time."

"How are they taking advantage of me?"

"They shouldn't drug you like this."

"Woof woof," echoes in the background.

"Do you hear that barking? Is there a dog in here," I ask Eric as I look around for the animal?

"Summer, there's no dog in here. Would you like me to take you to your room? You don't have to wait for Rosa."

Embarrassment flushes through me. "Maybe it would be best for me to go back."

"Let me put the tray away, and I'll be back," Eric says as he picks up our trays.

A few tables down, the Brunswick Bullies look over at me, and I see smiles and hear giggles. I should have stayed in my room. Whitney walks up to the table and sits down.

"I just came over to check on you. I know I was short the last time we talked, but sometimes I get really claustrophobic in here with everyone. Too many emotions."

I nod. She looks at me with worried eyes as Eric approaches from behind her.

"Ready to go?"

I give him a nod, and he walks around to me and takes the locks off the wheelchair.

"They shouldn't drug her like that," Whitney says to Eric.

"I was thinking the exact same thing. She's not a danger to anyone or herself. She hasn't tried to do anything violent. It doesn't make sense," Eric says as he turns and pushes me away.

I close my eyes, and the ride flows. It seems never-ending and relaxing this time. Eric pushes me close to the windows, and I open my eyes from time to time and take a peep out. The wind must be blowing because the branches and leaves sway back and forth. The sun is brilliant and spread evenly with the beautiful shapely clouds. A flock of birds glides just below the clouds, racing away from showers set to come.

Eric stops, bends down, and whispers, "Try not to take the medicine."

I nod, and we continue on our journey.

"Stop," Rosa calls out as we pass the nurse's station. Eric changes direction and walks over.

"I can take it from here," she tells Eric.

"Okay, sure," he replies. "Don't forget what I told you, Summer," he voices this low, so only I hear as he walks away.

"You're back fast. How was your breakfast?" Rosa asks.

"Fine," falls from my lips.

"It's time for your dose of medicine."

I think about what Eric told me. Rosa walks over with a tiny white paper cup and a plastic cup of water. She hands it to me.

I muster all my strength to speak. "Do I have to take them?"

"Yes. Dr. Mocker says they must be administered."

I put the pills in my mouth, and she watches. There's no way of getting around this, so I swallow.

"Now open your mouth."

I open my mouth and move my tongue around. When I think about it, she's never asked me to do that before.

"Let's get you in your room so you can rest," she says as she pushes me toward the room door.

"What time is my session?" I ask Rosa.

She looks down at her cheap plastic watch and says, "In about two hours, but really, whenever Dr. Mocker calls for you."

Rosa helps me get out of the wheelchair and walks me to the bed.

"Now you get some rest. Try to stay in bed. I would hate for you to fall."

I nod, and she pushes the wheelchair out of the room and closes the door behind her.

I was looking forward to my session with Dr. Mocker, but I'm unsure if I can fully communicate my thoughts to him. It's like an enormous early morning dew covers my thoughts, slowly clearing and then fighting its way back. A massive yawn roars out my mouth, and once again, my eyes become heavy, and away I drift.

SESSION WITH DR. MOCKER

"**W**ake up now. It's time for your session with the doctor," Rosa says as she shakes my arm. I halfway open my eyes, then close them again.

"Wake up! Wake up now!" she says, shaking me again. My heavy eyelids rise and fall, rise and fall. I can fully hear her, and I try to force myself to wake up, but sleep sits heavily upon my mind.

"I don't know why they give you such a large dosage. It's going to be hard to keep you lucid," Rosa says while standing over me.

I finally fully open my eyes, and Rosa adjusts the bed so that I'm sitting up. She then pulls a phone out of her pocket and dials a number.

"Hey, Dr. Mocker," there is a pause, and then "Summer is out of it. She's extremely drowsy and unable to keep her eyes open. I think we should just let her sleep." A pause follows, and then she responds to him, "Okay, no problem," and then she hangs up the phone.

"Okay, Summer. Let's fix this cover for you. Dr. Mocker will be doing an in-room visit today and is coming here now."

Rosa adjusts the cover and tucks it around me. She then enters the bathroom and comes back with a wet towel.

"Let's wipe your face off." She dabs the cold towel against my forehead and then rolls it over my eyes and cheeks.

"Would you like a drink of water?"

"Coffee," I tell her and manage a short laugh.

"Good idea. Let me try to find some," Rosa says, then exits the room.

My mind drifts in and out of wakefulness. I'm in a tall grassy field, and then I'm sitting up in a hospital bed. At times, what's real and a dream blend together to the point I'm unsure if I'm awake or sleeping. I stand in front of a house with bright orange and red flames erupting. Choking and gasping on the heavy fumes of smoke, full of horrendous fear, I turn and run away from the fire as fast as my feet can carry me. I don't look back. The further I get, the more my breathing returns to normal. I open my eyes, and Dr. Mocker sits in a chair beside my bed, holding a folder and a pen.

"How are you today?" he says with a gigantically enormous smile that warms up my spirit.

"Good." Good is always my go-to word, even when I'm feeling horrible and struck down with fear and confusion.

"I like to hear that from my patients. I hear you had an incident last night?"

"An incident?"

"Something in your room frightened you?"

"Oh, yes. Somehow, my bed was moving uncontrollably. Did Rosa, I mean, Ms. Charlie, tell you? She saw it happen."

"She didn't put it in her notes that she witnessed it, but I'm sure the bed was probably malfunctioning. She did write that you feel like your dead husband is haunting you?"

I search my mind for a response. I don't want him to think I'm crazy. What if the bed did malfunction and fear exaggerated it in my mind? The harder I try to think, the more the fog lifts.

"I don't quite remember," I lie.

"I have a question for you. Do you remember the night your husband died?"

It's a relief he didn't say, the night I murdered my husband. Maybe he thinks I didn't do it, too. That would be good. He can see I'm not crazy, I'm not a danger to myself or anyone else, and he can let me out of here.

"Summer? Summer?" he calls my name, and I look him in the eyes.

"Did you hear my question?" he asks.

"Why are you giving me this medication? I can barely function with it."

"To help you."

"By drugging me?"

Rosa walks into the room carrying a Styrofoam cup in her hand.

"I got you some coffee. I didn't know how you like it, so I made it the way I drink mine." She walks over. "Are you able to hold it? It's very hot."

"I can manage," I tell her as I grab the coffee out of her hand.

"Dr. Mocker, if you need me, I'll be at the nurse's station," Rosa says, and she walks out of the room.

I take a sip of the hot coffee. One thing for sure: Rosa likes her coffee extra sweet and creamy, but I like it. It warms me up and shakes a tiny bit of the grogginess away.

"Why are you giving me such strong drugs? I'm okay. The anxiety attack was last night. I don't think I need such strong medication that's gonna knock me out all day and night."

"Do you have a doctor's degree?" he asks with a smile.

What an asshole!

"I'm sorry, I didn't mean to say that," he says and rubs my arm.

In that moment, the stirring rage that resides in my body relaxes a little. His touch overwhelms me. His distasteful question erases from my mind. I've got a soft spot for this doctor. I should have been his wife. I search my mind for the questions I have for him.

"Dr. Mocker, did you know your wife worked for my husband?"

His eyes widen as his eyebrows go up, and he tilts his head slightly to the back.

"What!"

"Your wife worked for my husband."

"The medication could be causing you to create ideas in your mind."

"I've seen your picture on her desk."

"And where was this at?"

"They were having an affair."

"What?" he says as he sets his folder and pen down.

"How do you know this?"

"Well, I believe I walked in on them in bed together."

"You believe?"

"I'm unsure about my thoughts right now, as everything seems so foggy."

A few seconds of quietness passed between the doctor and me. He looks at me and rubs his chin as his face tenses up.

"What else do you think you remember?"

"I think she was pregnant with his baby, or maybe your baby."

"Pregnant, really?" He nods his head up and down. "Tell me more."

"I don't know anymore, but I was hoping maybe you did and could possibly tell me something. Maybe you noticed something strange with your wife?"

"Summer, I'm sorry, but I think maybe you have mistaken my wife for someone else. My wife didn't have a job."

"How did she die?"

"Summer, we will not be discussing my wife or any of my personal life."

The room becomes quiet, and the doctor picks up his paper and pen and scribbles, writing in his folder. I feel my eyelids slowly closing, then the doctor's folder slams down on my leg near the foot of the bed.

"Summer? Summer, do you think you remember anything else?"

My eyelids jump open, then fall back down. He takes the coffee cup out of my hand.

Stay awake, stay awake, I tell myself.

Frustration floods my body, I want to discuss more but my body disobeys and my mind keeps going in and out..

"I have another session, so I've got to go. Get some rest." He gets up and reaches for his folder and pen. Papers fall out of the folder, landing all over the floor. It startles me out of my doze. Dr. Mocker squats down and begins picking them up. I look over at the floor and can see a small picture of me, my name on the top of many of the documents, then the words "paranoid schizophrenia with narcissistic rage" written on one of the papers. Dr. Mocker quickly grabs all the papers, stands, and turn to leave the room. He accidentally leaves the door cracked open, and I can hear him talking to Rosa.

"She's delusional, thinks her deceased husband is haunting her. She also thinks she knew my wife. Let's put her on the schedule for another ECT."

"Are you sure that's necessary?"

"Yes, schedule it for as soon as possible."

"No problem, Dr. Mocker."

WHAT THE HELL! I can't do another session of ECT. I've got to talk to Whitney. Was the memory a part of my imagination? I lay in bed, and my mind races to sleep.

WRONG DIAGNOSIS

wakening with stiffness and prickly legs, the evening sun lets in bright white radiant strands of light. The clock on the wall says 6:02. Nobody woke me for lunch, but it's okay. I needed sleep, and dinner has just begun. My mind is so much more alert with clearer thoughts. Hunger churns my stomach, and I'm ready to eat. I stand up, and it causes dizziness to overwhelm me, so I sit back down. On my nightstand sits a cup of half-drunk cold coffee. I grab it, gulp it down, wait a few minutes, and try to get up again. This time, I feel a little more stable and less dizzy. Walking out the door, the halls are bare. Everyone must already be in the cafeteria.

I pass the nurse's desk, and Rosa is sitting behind the desk, looking down at a computer. She looks up and asks, "Summer, are you okay with walking by yourself?"

"Yes, I think so," I tell her as I stagger a few steps.

"Let me push you to the cafe. I would hate to see you fall."

"No, I can make it."

"Summer, I would get fired if you fall. You've been on some very heavy medication. Please wait there while I get the wheelchair." She gets up, walks into a closet, and returns seconds later, pushing a wheelchair. I sit down. She comes in front to put my feet up, then returns behind me to start pushing me. Unlike the casual pace that Eric pushed me earlier, she goes at a fast pace.

"Rosa?"

"Yes, Summer?"

"Am I going to get any more of the medication you gave me earlier?"

"Yes. Dr. Mocker has you taking it every six hours until further notice."

"Why am I being given such strong medicine?"

"That's a question for the doctor."

"Is there a library here or anywhere I can use the computer?"

"No, I'm sorry. There are no libraries or computers where you can access the Internet."

"Can you tell me the name of the medication the doctor is prescribing me?"

"Haloperidol and Alprazolam."

We ride the rest of the way in quietness. I'm hoping to see Eric and Whitney in the cafeteria. Maybe one of them can tell me about this medication . We enter the doors of the cafeteria, and it's full. Rosa takes me to get my food and asks me where I would like to sit. I scan the room until I see Eric, then point in his direction.

"You and Eric are pretty friendly," Rosa says as if insinuating something.

"I guess," I reply as I roll my eyes.

She pushes me over to his table.

"Will you take her to her room after dinner?"

"Of course," Eric says with a huge smile running across his face. Rosa turns and walks off.

"You're looking better. You were out of it earlier," Eric says.

"Sleep and coffee," I say with a laugh.

Eric shoves broccoli into his mouth. I'm surprised to see him eating broccoli because, normally, he's always eating junk.

"How's the broccoli?"

"Eatable."

We both laugh.

"I put on a few pounds, and I've got to stay in shape for the ladies," Eric says, smiling.

"I knew you were a playboy."

"Naw, actually, I'm not, and I like my women a little older and with a little melanin," he tells me with another adorable smile and a wink.

"Eric, Eric, Eric, where is this coming from?"

"Just putting it out there."

We both laugh. Eric is such a cute flirt.

I look up from Eric's bright green eyes and see Whitney. We make eye contact, and I beckon for her to come over to the table.

"Summer, I'm happy to see you alert. This morning you were barely here," Whitney says as she approaches the table.

"Well, I really need you guys' help and advice. Whatever you can lend."

"What's wrong?" Whitney asks.

"I'll probably be out of it again very soon. I'm pretty sure when I get back, I'm going to get another dosage of medication. Rosa told me Dr. Mocker wants me to be drugged every six hours with Haloperidol and Alprazolam."

"Yeah, you're going to be out of it," Eric says.

"I don't understand why they keep drugging you like that. They had you drugged up before a few weeks ago."

"Normally, they drug people for being violent. That's why I asked you this morning what you did!" Eric exclaims.

"At least they don't have her in a straitjacket," Whitney says.

"Well, they are going to give me ECT in a few days, and I don't want it."

"ECT? Why? Something is not right," says Eric.

I shrug.

"Eric, I was hoping you could talk to your dad about my case and find out as much information as possible. I don't have any money to pay him, but any little information he offers would be greatly appreciated.

I pause, trying to gather my thoughts.

"Whitney, was the memory I had the other night real, or could it have been my imagination?"

"That's like asking if Marie Laveau really lived. Of course it's real. Didn't it seem real?"

"Well, the memory was of me catching my husband in the bed with his secretary, and guess who his secretary was?"

They look in anticipation.

"It was Dr. Mocker's wife, Christina Mocker."

"Wait a minute, let me get this right," Eric begins saying with raised eyebrows and a half-smile on his face. "You had a dream your husband was cheating with Dr. Mocker's wife?"

"Not exactly. Whitney came to my room the other night. I did a session with her, and she was able to help me remember catching my husband with Dr. Mocker's wife."

Eric puts his hand over his mouth, and lines appear on the corners of his face, revealing a smile hiding behind his hand. It seems Eric has a flare for drama, or maybe he's just bored.

"I asked Dr. Mocker about it, and he said it wasn't true. He claims his wife didn't work. I didn't think to ask whether her name was Christina or not."

"Maybe he didn't know his wife was working," says Whitney.

"That's definitely a possibility," I answer.

"Isn't it a coincidence how your husband is dead and Dr. Mocker's wife is dead?" Eric says as he looks at me with a tilted head and suspicion in his eyes. Whitney looks over at Eric. I hear a noise under the table, and Eric reaches down and rubs his leg. She must have kicked him to be quiet.

"Dr. Mocker thinks I'm delusional. I need to prove to him I'm not before the ECT session."

"Whitney, I need you to help me remember as much as possible, and Eric, please talk to your dad?"

"It's hard to get calls around here, but I'll try my best," Eric says.

"It's all going to work out," Whitney says as she nibbles on a hard, dry roll.

"I sure hope so because this is my life at stake."

"Whitney," my voice becomes a little shaky from nervousness.

"Yes, Summer?"

"You say you can talk to spirits, right? Can you contact Charles?"

Whitney drops her shoulders and purses her lips. "It doesn't quite work like that. They have to be open to being contacted. Charles may not want to be disturbed, and some spirits that died violent deaths can have violent, aggressive spirits. I just don't recommend it."

"Just thought I would ask."

We spend the rest of dinner eating and discussing frivolous stuff. Like why they always play the Golden Girls on the TV in the dayroom and how many people they have watching the cameras. I look around and realize the cafeteria is almost empty.

"Would you like for me to take you to your room?" Eric asks.

"I can definitely walk now," I tell him as I stand up and pick up my tray.

"How about I walk with you, just in case?"

"Sure, Eric."

Whitney smiles and says, "I guess I'll walk with the Lord and with the cameras."

We all laugh.

After I dump my tray, I come back for the wheelchair, then Eric and I begin walking.

"You know, there really is something very off about your whole situation. Honestly, no one else has received ECT since I've been here. I didn't even know they still did that. No offense, but I thought of it as being some type of ancient treatment that they did to extremely crazy people. None of my interactions with you have shown you to be crazy or anything."

"Well, Dr. Mocker said that's what the judge ordered after I repeatedly tried to commit suicide, but I don't remember any of it."

"It must be horrible, losing your memory like that."

"You have no idea."

We approach the nurse's station, and Rosa is sitting down, eyes glued to the computer screen.

"See you in the morning," Eric says as he turns and walks away.

Eric is such a sweet guy, and I can't believe he was flirting with me. I go into my room and take my shoes off to prop my feet up on the bed. It would be nice to have a TV here. I reach into the nightstand, pull out the notebook Dr. Mocker gave me, and begin writing.

Someone knocks on the door and then pushes it open. Rosa walks in with the pills and water cup. Taking a deep breath and blowing out frustration, all I can do is shake my head. I absolutely, positively don't want to be drugged.

"Did you have a good dinner?"

"Yes, I did. Do I have to take these pills?"

"Summer, I'm sorry, but I have to give them to you and make sure you're taking them."

"What if I refuse to take them?"

"We would have to administer them with a needle."

Rosa hands me the cups. I take the pills, put them in my mouth, and take a swallow of water.

"Okay, open up." Rosa looks into my mouth. "Good job," she says and walks out.

I rush to the bathroom, look in the mirror, and stick my fingers down my throat as far as they'll go. I gag and gag again. Sure enough,

I vomited up everything I ate at dinner and the pills Rosa just made me take. Stress lifts off my mind; I don't want to be drugged anymore.

Undressing, I look in the mirror at my body. I've definitely lost weight since I've been here. If I have to throw up multiple times a day, it's not going to help. I turn the shower on and get in. The cold water hitting me causes me to shiver, but it slowly warms up and begins to feel so good and relaxing.

Paranoid schizophrenia with narcissistic rage . . . that can't be me. I can be a little paranoid at times, but isn't everyone?

Schizophrenia? I don't hear voices or have any other personalities.

As far as narcissism goes, that's impossible! I loved Charles more than I loved myself, I don't have any type of self-entitlement personality, and I'm not a person who has episodes of rage.

I know Dr. Mocker is the "doctor," but he got my diagnosis wrong.

DAYROOM

've just awoken, and breakfast is about to end. I wish I had an alarm clock. Normally, someone will knock on the door and announce mealtime. They keep very strict eating hours around here. I think it helps them to keep track of everyone. Maybe they didn't knock on my door because they assumed I would be out of it. I still can't believe Delisa woke me in the middle of the night to take a dosage of medicine. Thank God someone started knocking on the walls in their room when she handed me the pills, and she had to go check on them. The pills now rest among many others in my nightstand, nestled between two big pairs of cotton panties.

I slip into some jogging pants and a T-shirt, then leave to try to catch Whitney and Eric before they leave the breakfast area.

When I arrive, only a few stragglers sit in the cafeteria. At a table to themselves sit Whitney and Eric. My appetite disappears, and I run over.

"Good morning, guys," I say as they look at each other, smiling.

"You guys seem happy."

"More along the lines of full of enthusiasm. We've been sitting in here waiting for you."

"Well, I'm here."

"I was able to find out some information last night," says Eric, shaking his head up and down.

"Well, what are you waiting for?"

"Your husband died in a house fire with a Christina Mocker."

My breath runs out of my body, and my hand reaches up, covering my mouth. Inhaling and then exhaling, I gain composure.

"Oh, my goodness! So, that memory wasn't a delusional dream. I'm not crazy!" I exclaim.

Whitney and Eric look at me as if waiting for me to say more.

"Oh, wait, did I kill them both?" I ask.

"Both their bodies had multiple stab wounds. So they were stabbed, and then the house was set on fire," says Eric.

I shake my head, picturing the gruesome scene. The picture is too vivid, bloody bodies lying in the living room, my hands and clothes covered in blood, flames taking over the house, engulfing my furniture and belongings, while I watch in satisfaction. Pleased to see my husband and his mistress turn to ash. I shake my head as if trying to throw the images out of my mind.

"Summer, you didn't do it," Whitney tells me.

"How do you know?" I ask her.

"Marie told me it wasn't you."

"Well, did she say who it was?"

"No, it doesn't work like that."

"So, how?"

"Spirits can't tell us what we need to figure out ourselves."

"I don't know about this, Marie. My mom would make me pray to her, and I always believed in her, but where has it gotten me? She could be a figment of our imagination, causing us to have these supernatural thoughts and causing the doctors to think we're crazy. I think it'd be best if we don't discuss Marie. I need substantial information and evidence that will exonerate me and get me out of here and back with my daughter. You guys are smiling like it's good news, but it's horrible news. They think I killed two people."

"Listen, Summer, think about this. How could you," Eric looks me up and down, "stab and kill two people at one time? Each body had been stabbed over twenty times. One would have gotten away. I'm with Whitney. You did not do this."

"Eric, how did you find out this information?"

"I called my dad, and he told me. He's supposed to do a little research to try to get more information."

One of the guards who monitor the cafeteria walks up to us and asks us to leave. I look around, and we're the only ones inside.

"Let's continue this talk in the dayroom," I say to them.

We get up, deposit our trays, and head out.

Eric stops walking and says, "Guys, what if Dr. Mocker did it?"

A smile runs across my face, and then I burst into laughter. "That sounds ludicrous!" I say.

"Actually, it's not too farfetched. Just imagine he finds out his wife is having an affair with your husband. He kills them both, then puts the murders on you," says Whitney.

"Whitney, you're psychic. Tell us what happened?" I say.

"Once again, I don't like that word, psychic, and I only know what I'm told."

"Well, can your spirit friends tell us if it was him?"

Eric looks at Whitney and me and shakes his head.

"I think he did it," Eric says.

"I don't!" I exclaim.

"Why are you getting upset? Think about it," Whitney says.

"You get locked up, you somehow end up in here under his care, and as soon as you get here, he starts giving you ECT. He's trying to cover something up."

"And don't forget how they are always drugging her," Eric says to Whitney.

"Dr. Mocker is so nice, and I just can't fathom that," I tell them.

They probably think I'm naïve, but I've been in multiple sessions with Dr. Mocker, and he doesn't seem like the type of person to do something like that. He seems gentle and kind. He understands me and wants to help me; maybe Christina isn't his wife. Maybe the last name is a coincidence.

"Eric, did you find out Dr. Mocker's wife's name?" I ask.

"No, the article my dad read to me didn't list a spouse or any relatives of Christina, but we should be able to ask a staff member. I'm sure they go to Christmas parties together," Eric says as he laughs and puts his middle finger up to a camera.

Mr. Clean stands in the hallway by the dayroom doors. He shoots Eric a stern look.

"Hey, Carl, do you know Dr. Mocker's wife's name?" Eric asks Mr. Clean

"What wife?"

"His dead wife," Eric says as he walks toward Carl.

"Get out of my face before I make you go to your room."

"That's rude. Just asking a question, man."

"You're either in the dayroom or in your room. Pick one."

Eric picks the dayroom.

We walk in and look for a place away from everyone. The dayroom is a huge room with lots of brightness from plentiful windows. It has a few worn-out couches and lots of tables and chairs. The couches are always full. There is a bookcase that holds no books. From what I've heard, it used to have books and magazines until someone got mad and started throwing the books, and a staff member got hit in the head. A big television sits high on the wall. Sometimes, they have movie days and play movies, but not often because everyone argues about which movie to watch. There are cameras at the door when you walk in, in every corner of the room, and at the door when you walk out. Two staff members sit in the dayroom at all times. They're normally on their phones, which, from what I heard, they aren't supposed to have or be watching the television like the rest of us. I hate the dayroom. There is always someone screaming, fighting, or being annoying. Also, the Brunswick Bullies are always hanging out in there, and I try to avoid them at all costs.

We notice all the tables with chairs are taken, but we see chairs scattered throughout the room. We gather them and go sit in the back of the room near the windows. It seems a little awkward between me, Whitney, and Eric. It's just hard for me to believe Dr. Mocker is behind me being in here.

"When is your next session with Dr. Mocker?" Eric asks.

"Probably tomorrow, which is also my birthday. I can't believe I'll be spending my birthday in this place."

"Oh wow, how old will you be?" Eric asks.

"I'll never tell," I say with a laugh.

I look over and see Rosa scanning the room. We make eye contact, and she walks over.

"There's Rosa coming to give someone some medicine," says an older gray-haired lady that's sitting a few feet away.

Rosa approaches me and tells me it's time for my medicine. Eric and Whitney look at me, seeking a response. I comply by taking the pill cup and water.

"Hey, Rosa."

"Hey, Eric."

"Looking out the window, it seems like it's a nice day outside, is it?" Eric asks her.

"It's pretty nice, but I don't get to enjoy it because I'm working," Rosa says as she turns away from me and faces Eric.

I take the pills out of the pill cup and tuck them into my seat cushion, then take a swallow of the water. The older gray-haired lady watches me, smiling. Rosa turns back toward me and asks me to open my mouth. I open it and show her under my tongue. She takes the water cup and walks back out.

"Can I have those pills?" asks the gray-haired lady.

"Sure," I tell her, retrieving them from the dirty seat cushion. I hand them over to her, and she takes them. Whitney, Eric, and I look at each other and laugh.

"Summer, they are going to know you're not taking your medicine. You're going to have to pretend like you are," Whitney tells me.

"Maybe I should pretend to be too tired to eat lunch and skip it. Then I can act drowsy at dinner. Maybe make them push me to dinner. What do you guys think?"

"That could work," says Eric.

This is an insane situation, but I will figure it out, and at least now I have two friends who want to help. The gray-haired lady moves her chair closer to us.

"If you get any more pills, give them to me, okay?" she whispers with a huge grin.

"Sure," I tell her.

Whitney, Eric, and I shoot each other another glance.

"Did I hear you guys talking about Dr. Mocker?" asks the gray-haired lady.

"Not really," Eric replies.

"He's a cutie," she says.

"I think it's time I go to my room. I'm feeling a little drowsy," I tell the group as I wink at them. I get up and walk out of the room. I can feel eyes watching me as I pass through the doorways.

"Where are you headed?" asks Carl.

I manage a fake yawn and tell him I'm going to my room. He gets up and follows a few steps behind until I reach the nurse's station, where Rosa sits.

"Rosa, is my next ECT scheduled?"

Her eyebrows come together, and she looks at me for a few moments before speaking.

"How did you know we were scheduling a session?"

"Dr. Mocker told me," I lie.

"It's in three days."

"Is ECT a procedure that's done a lot here?"

Rosa looks at me and cocks her head to the side. She gets up from the desk and walks closer to me. In a low voice, she tells me,

"I've been a nurse for over fifteen years, and this is the first time I've ever witnessed someone receive ECT."

"Why me?"

"That's a question for your doctor."

"Does it seem suspicious?"

"Suspicious how?"

I'm unsure how to respond. If I told her I thought the doctor could have killed my husband and his wife and made me take the fall for it, I might look crazy, but maybe she will believe me and help me.

"Rosa, I really would like to talk to you. Can you come to my room?"

"Sure, I can. Give me a minute."

Rosa makes a call for another nurse to come to the desk. I walk to my room and wait for her. If she can listen and possibly understand, then maybe she can see that I'm not crazy and there's more to my story. Also, if something funny is happening here, maybe she can get it to the outside world and help exonerate me. Rosa knocks on the door and walks in. I sit on my bed Indian style and begin telling her about my memory of catching Charles and Christina, and then I mention how they were murdered together. I leave out how the memory came about. Rosa listens without any interruptions. As I talk, I can see her nodding her head in agreement and making facial expressions that look like she might believe what I'm telling her.

"So, what do you think about it?" I ask her.

"Summer, that's a lot of information for me to process, but first off, according to Delisa, Dr. Mocker's wife died of cancer."

My airways close, I lose my breath for a few seconds, then they reopen. Absolutely speechless. I don't want Dr. Mocker to be the villain, but I don't want to be the murderer, either. Rosa looks at me with sad eyes. Pity is not what I'm seeking at the moment.

"Why is he giving me the ECT then?! Why me!" I cry out in a loud burst of sadness. I'm trying to hold it together, but at this moment, it's impossible. Warm tears roll down my cheeks uncontrollably. Rosa embraces me, and her hand gently rubs my back.

"I'm sorry, dear. I don't know why you're getting the ECT, but I'm sure he thinks it's what you need. Dr. Mocker is a great doctor."

We stay in this position for what seems like an eternity. The warmth of her body comforts me, so I close my eyes and pray.

Lord God, I haven't come to you in a long time, but please help me not get the next ECT treatment and help me to remember everything that happened.

"Rosa, last week, you said Dr. Mocker likes the ladies. Why did you say that?"

Rosa looks me in the eyes, and I can tell she's debating whether she should lie or be truthful.

"I caught him having an affair with a staff member."

BIRTHDAY AT BRUNSWICK

My body shivers profusely, waking me to a new day. Why is this place so freezing cold, and the covers never stay on me? Do I sleep that badly? Pulling the cover up around me, I remember today, February seventh, is my birthday, and I dread spending it here without Charles. The rest of my birthdays will be without him. It's funny how you plan on spending your life with a person and think you'll grow old together, then you kill them and feel all alone. Crazy how life is, or maybe just my life. Let me cut these pitiful 'woe is me' thoughts off. It's my birthday, for heaven's sake.

I can still remember my best birthday as if it were yesterday. I had turned seven, and my parents threw a big block party for me. The tables were lined with delicious homemade fruit pastries. A massive pot of gumbo sat right in the center of one of the tables. My mother made the best chicken and sausage gumbo. The aroma would capture the whole neighborhood, drawing people in like vultures to a carcass. My grandad played his fiddle, and my uncle sang blues songs on his guitar. We all swayed to the music. Aunt Lottie got so drunk that she started dropping to the floor and shaking her booty like a teenager. I'll never forget that day. Not like I forgot the day I murdered Charles.

"Bad thoughts of Charles's murder, please get out of my head."

I jump out of bed and head to the bathroom to freshen up. Today is going to be a happy day, I tell myself, trying to evoke positive vibes into the atmosphere. The cool water flows down my body in the shower, awakening me to the new morning. I shampoo my hair with coconut-scented shampoo. The aroma seeps into my mind as the water massages my scalp. I hold my head back, loving the feel of the drops beating against my body. I feel so calm and relaxed like I'm on a tropical island under a waterfall. I let the stream roll down my breasts and split down my nipples, imagining a handsome, muscular man's fingers lightly caressing my body.

My mind is made up. This place might be hell, but I'm going to make the most of it. Mind over matter. Whatever I allow my mind to think can be my reality, and at this moment, I'm in a tropical paradise, enjoying nature's beauty. Closing my eyes, I can see the brilliant white clouds sliding across the pale blue sky and the beaming sun piercing through, looking down at me, giving life to my soul. I turn and let the water hit my backside. The warmth rolls down my shoulders and back, drowning the negative fields and bringing my aura to life. Blissful, peaceful thoughts of another life with a loving husband and children in a beautiful house on Lake Pontchartrain come to my thoughts. I smile.

My daydream is suddenly interrupted by a knock on my door.

"Breakfast," I hear one of the staff members yell. I turn off the water and get out. Looking at myself in the mirror turns me on— the round firmness of my breasts, my hourglass figure, my hair wet and wavy. The dream of Dr. Mocker plays in my mind. I want him like I've never wanted a man before. I can't even remember the last time I had sex. I shake my head, trying to dismiss the sensual thoughts. This is the same man that has me scheduled for ECT. My stomach starts talking, and it's naming sweet breakfast treats. I slide my pants and shirt on, then head to the cafe. I figure since today is my birthday, I'm going to splurge. I'll definitely be getting pancakes with lots of butter, a little syrup, and enough bacon and sausage to make a piglet.

As soon as I walk into the cafe, I spot Dr. Mocker's fine ass. He's sitting with another one of the doctors, and they look like they are engaging in an interesting conversation. I get my tray and begin piling food on it. I walk over to the juice bar and get a cup of orange juice. I don't see Whitney or Eric, so I sit at an empty table by myself. The pancakes are steaming hot, and I put lots of butter on them. My mouth waters with the smell. I cut them into small pieces and begin eating. They are delicious. Fluffy, buttery, and just the right amount of sweetness.

I'm so into the pancakes I don't even notice when someone places a card on the table beside my plate. I look up and see Dr. Mocker walking away. So many things begin flooding my mind. Should I open it now or wait until later? Is it a special note? I quickly pick it up and open it. It's a birthday card. It has a picture of the sun shining and reads: Happy Birthday. I hope your day is filled with sunshine. How sweet of him! How did he know today was my birthday? I didn't even mention it in any of the sessions. I guess he read it in my file. He probably gives a card to every patient on their birthday.

Eric walks up and sits in front of me.

"How was your night?" he asks.

"Crappy. I found out Dr. Mocker's wife died from cancer. So, the Christina that was sleeping with Charles is a different Christina. Eric, it is not easy when you can't trust your thoughts."

"Oh wow! I guess you were right. Maybe Dr. Mocker didn't do it. What's that in the envelope?"

"A birthday card from the doctor."

"What doctor, Dr. Mocker?"

"Yes," I say with a smile.

"Well, happy birthday! Hey, if you want a drink later, I have some Jack Daniels in my room," Eric whispers in a voice so low that I can barely make out the words.

"What?! How?!"

"I have my ways."

Eric opens multiple packets of syrup and drenches his pancakes and sausage.

"How nice of the doctor to give you a card. No one gave me a card on my birthday."

"I guess I'm special."

"Well, Dr. Mocker does have a way with the ladies, I hear."

"That's weird. Rosa said the same thing. Why do you say that?" I ask Eric.

"Honestly, I don't know. I'm just repeating what I heard," he says as he stuffs a fork full of syrupy pancake into his mouth.

"From who?"

"I overheard some of the staff talking. Sometimes they talk around me. I don't ask questions. I just listen."

I finish the last of my orange juice and listen to Eric talk about partying on Bourbon Street. I've never been much of a party girl. I'm a homebody, and I think that's what Charles loved about me. He never had to guess where I was. I was either at work or home or maybe at the grocery store. I have always lived a simple life. I rarely drank and never did any non-prescription drugs. I love good books and documentaries about ancient times. Most people consider me a good ole' country girl—a southern charm. It doesn't take much to impress or please me.

"Want to come get a drink now?"

"It's too early for me," I tell Eric with a laugh.

"I really enjoy talking to you."

"I enjoy talking to you, too, Eric."

Eric gets up to take his tray and walks away. I guess Eric really does have a little crush on me. It's kind of funny. He's younger than me, and we're just not on the same page, but it's cute. Across the room, I can see Carl staring my way out of the corner of my eye. I don't like that guy. Gathering my tray and cup, I walk over and dump them and proceed to my room.

As I sit in my room writing in my journal, I'm startled by Carl walking through the door of my room; he never knocks like most of the other staff. He's just rude and looks evil. He walks like a stick is constantly shoved up his ass. "Dr. Mocker requested you come early," he tells me. My heart lights up to hear Dr. Mocker's name. I guess I have a little crush on the doctor. I can't help it. Carl stands with his back against the open door and watches me as I walk to the bathroom.

Looking in the mirror, I wish I had some makeup, a curling iron, or at least some lip gloss. Some of the other patients have makeup, but their family members bring it to them. I brush my hair back, redo my ponytail, and walk out of the bathroom.

"Don't keep the doctor waiting. He's a busy man," Carl says.

My eyes roll, and I walk past Carl to Dr. Mocker's office.

As I pass the dayroom, I see Eric sitting at a table by himself, reading a book. I never took Eric for much of a reader. Carl and I continue walking to the end of the hall. This is a pretty big building, and I can only remember this one floor. We're not allowed to leave this floor, and you must have a keycard to leave the big white doors that lead to the rest of the building. This floor has its own cafeteria, but I never see any food being cooked. I think they cook the food elsewhere and bring it to this floor. A nurse's station is on both ends of the floor, and the dayroom is right in the middle. As I approach the doctor's office, I see the door is cracked. I look up, smile at the camera, and knock. The door opens slightly with each knock.

"Come on in, Summer." Dr. Mocker is standing up with his back to the door. He's holding an open manila folder. "Have a seat while I gather a few items," he tells me.

He puts the folder down and walks over to a closet. He pulls out a big red-looking lunchbox. "We're going outside today."

My face lights up. Outside! He pulls his keycard from his desk and slips it in his pocket, then takes his jacket and puts it on. I watch, admiring his poise.

"Thank you for the card."

"No problem. I keep cards for every occasion in my desk and give them out here and there."

I guess it wasn't a special card. He picks up his notebook and a pen, then opens the lunchbox and lays them on top.

"We can head out now."

Eagerly, I get up and follow behind the doctor. We walk down the hall at a steady pace. No words pass between us. The doctor stops at the nurse's station and tells a nurse I don't recognize that we would be having our session on the patio. Then, we proceed to the double doors. He scans his badge, and the doors slowly open to a long hallway. Natural sunlight pours in from the windows lining the corridor. We walk to the end and make a left to go to an elevator.

"How has your day been going?" Dr. Mocker asks as he scans his badge again and presses the button on the elevator.

"It was going okay, but now that I get to venture out, I don't quite know."

We step onto the elevator, and I see the building has four floors. He swipes his card, presses the "1" button, and we begin descending. We reach the first floor and get off. I can see a station with what looks like security guards sitting to the left. Dr. Mocker tells me we will be leaving through a side exit that leads to a patio. The bottom floor of the building is nice-looking, with lots of faux plants and a sitting area. We pass a few offices, but few people are in the hallways. We approach a glass door, and he scans his badge again and opens the door.

The cool, fresh breeze rushes me. What a beautiful day! I take in everything God has created; the grass looks crisp and green, and the trees dominate their surroundings, spreading their limbs and showing off the beautiful pine cones and needles. Glancing at the sky takes my breath away. I inhale the smell of nature. It's crazy how grateful

I am at this very moment. We take going outside for granted, but the minute we're told we can't go out, it makes outside appear impressive.

"Thank you for bringing me out," I tell Dr. Mocker.

He leads me to a red plastic bench that connects to a table. We sit down.

"I thought it would do you good to get some fresh air, and today is your birthday, so I arranged this outing," says Dr. Mocker.

He begins opening the red lunchbox. "I have a special treat for you."

"Really?" I say, smiling like a schoolgirl.

He pulls out a plastic container and hands it to me.

"Thank you," I say before even opening the container. I don't know what to think. As I slowly pull the lid, the scent of cream cheese, butter, and sugar seeps out. I close my eyes for a split second, pull the lid completely off, then open my eyes again. Inside the container is a giant cupcake with white icing swirled on top.

"It looks delicious," I say and begin taking it out.

"Wait," Dr. Mocker says, and he pulls out a small candle. He sticks it in the cupcake, takes a lighter out of his pocket, and lights it.

"Happy birthday, Summer James."

I blow out the candle and wish to be anywhere else and in the doctor's arms. No longer can I take it; I bite into the cupcake.

"Red velvet, my favorite!" I tell Dr. Mocker.

"We have something in common. That's my favorite as well. There is a new bakery around the corner from here. They just opened about two weeks ago. I usually stop there every morning before coming in."

"Didn't you tell me you were on a special diet?"

"I am, but the bakery has delicious coffee."

Curiosity is getting the best of me, so I have to ask, "Dr. Mocker, do you do this for all your patients?"

"Only the special ones."

"So I am a special one?"

My question lingers and goes unanswered. I continue to eat like a fat kid. Sweets are my weakness.

"You look like you're enjoying yourself," Dr. Mocker says.

"I am."

"Would you like a bottle of water?"

"Yes, thank you."

He takes a small bottle of water out of the lunch box and hands it to me. "How have you been feeling?"

"Good . . . even better now that you have treated me to my favorite dessert."

"You don't feel drowsy?"

"No, I feel fine," I tell Dr. Mocker, and then I remember the pills I'm supposed to be taking makes me drowsy. He watches me as I eat.

"Well, I do feel drowsy at times, but I think the excitement of coming out is giving me energy."

"Have any memories started returning?"

"No."

He shakes his head and then asks me, "Are you having any dreams?"

"Not that I remember."

"There is a trail that goes around the building. Would you like to walk it?"

"Sure," I say as I stuff the last piece of cupcake in my mouth.

He gets up from the table, leaving his things. We begin walking through the grass toward a dirt path. A small wooden sign that reads

Brunswick Nature Trail sticks up out of the ground. Grass grows across the trail and appears as if it's seldom walked. The trees are plentiful and the size of skyscrapers. They line each side of the trail. Colorful wildflowers dance along the path as the wind gently blows. The sunbeams and surrounds us with heat, which feels so good. I lift my face to the sky and let the rays pour on me.

"What would you like to talk about?" Dr. Mocker asks me.

"Nothing in particular. I'm just enjoying being out."

Not only am I enjoying being out, but I'm also enjoying being in the presence of Dr. Mocker. This walk actually feels a little romantic. I wonder if he thinks the same thing. We walk at a slow, steady pace. I begin twirling around. Dr. Mocker looks at me in astonishment.

"Are you okay?"

"According to you guys, I'm crazy, right?"

Dr. Mocker doesn't respond.

"I'm enjoying the beauty in the world. I want to take advantage of being out here on this warm summer's day."

He laughs, and it melts my heart. What is it about this man?

"Twirl me around," I tell him, and he grabs my hand and begins spinning me. His touch feels good. No words pass from us, but emotion flows in the air. I spin while looking from him to the sky. My heart is happy, and my mind is at peace. This is what living is all about, simple, peaceful moments, enjoying nature's beauty.

As I spin around, I trip on a small stick that was apparently in the path. Dr. Mocker's grip tightens on my hand. His strength does not save us. We both go down, me first and him on top of me. His body feels heavy and hard like he often goes to the gym. We look each other in the eyes. His beautiful greenish-hazel eyes stir my hormones. He smiles, and I laugh; it must be contagious because elaborate laughter explodes from him. This makes me laugh even more. The laughter slowly ceases, and he just lays there, not breaking his stare. I want to kiss him, but before I can make my mind up, he gets up and extends his hand toward me. He pulls me up with one arm. I admire his strength. However, he wasn't strong enough to keep us from falling. We dust off our clothes.

"Are you okay?" he asks me.

"You ask me that a lot," I say.

"Well, my goal is for you and all my patients to be as comfortable here as possible."

All his patients, I think. I guess that means all his patients get this treatment.

"I'm okay, and I appreciate your consideration." He smiles his fantastic smile.

"Are you ready to continue our walk, or do you need a minute?"

"My ankle feels a little sore." Of course, I'm lying, but I would say anything to prolong this walk.

"Let me take a look at it." He squats down, looks at my ankle, and runs his hand over it.

"Does this hurt?" he asks.

"Yes, a little," I lie, trying to look as if I'm in pain.

"I can go get a wheelchair if you can't walk back?"

"No, that's not necessary. I can walk if we keep a slow pace."

"We can walk slow. Put your arm around me, and I'll help support you."

I know he notices the smile that floods my face. I put my arm around the doctor, and we begin to walk together. His scent circulates in my nose, combining the smell of cedar wood, lavender, bergamot, and mint. It's so radiating. We slowly walk through the woods until we reach the end of the trail, which is actually the beginning of a new longing to survive this place. This birthday isn't too bad after all.

WHO'S THERE

Rain pours down outside my window, pounding on the windowsill. Thunder flashes and instantly lightens the sky for a few moments. The beautiful sounds of nature are so soothing. I curl up in my covers, relaxing. Nights here are always so lonely. For years, I slept next to Charles. Whether we were happy or horribly upset with each other, we always slept snuggled in each other. He would hold me in his arms, and I would feel his warm breath softly blowing up against my neck. My body would conform to his to the point it appeared like we were one. Now I have to sleep alone with the cold air from the air conditioner blowing down on me, always freezing my body.

Not only am I alone but trapped in my thoughts.

Trying to think only good things is sometimes so hard at times. The ECT session is approaching, and it tears at my tranquility. I would rather die than do it again and let it wipe my memory. Having to wake up not knowing where I am or how I got here. For now, I'll just focus on the rain and the thunder. I close my eyes and slowly drift to sleep.

Crrrrrrr... the sound of the door cracking open wakes me up from my light sleep. Looking up from under my sheet, a tall shadow stands by the foot of my bed. A warm hand glides its way up my leg, from my foot, then up to my calf. The outside lights don't reveal enough light for me to identify the person or being. Could this be Charles's restless spirit haunting me? I lay here a second to see if it goes away. If I make a big fuss and it's all in my head, that's more of a reason for them to give me the ECT. The figure comes closer, and the hand moves above my knees, nearing my thighs. Finally, I sit up, and the hand leaves my legs, but the figure comes closer and puts his hands on my shoulders, pushing me back down to the bed. It climbs up on top of me. Heavy breathing circulates in the air, and I can smell tobacco. He's a smoker—spirits can't smoke—this person is real.

"Get off me!" I scream.

The sounds of the door opening bounce off the walls, and another figure steps into the room, walking over to the bed.

"Helppppp!" I scream, and a hand covers my mouth.

"Help me hold her," says one of the figures.

The person that walked in tries to hold me, and my arms start swinging and throwing punching while my legs kick.

"She scratched me!" shrieks one of the shadows as my nails make contact with skin. A hand smacks my face and my entire cheek stings.

"We only have a few minutes. Hurry," comes a masculine voice in a whisper.

A hand makes its way to my crotch and starts trying to pull my pants down. My teeth clench down on the hand covering my mouth. He screams and starts slamming my head into the headboard. Throbs of pain circulate over the back of my head, and a muffled scream comes from my mouth.

"Shut the fuck up before I strangle you," says one of the shadows.

I continue to try to scream and bite. Dying doesn't seem all that bad at this moment. The sound of a zipper moving down rings in my ears, and I fight with everything I have, wiggling, twisting, turning, and trying to get the first figure off me.

One of the figures whispers very low, "I think we should leave."

The other guy moves on top of me, trying to get his pants down with one hand.

"Help, please, please, help," chokes out my mouth.

The man on top of me puts his hands around my throat, his grip firm and his hands strong. I quickly lose my breath. Pulling and pulling on the man's hands seems useless. What have I to fight for? Releasing the man's wrist, I let him choke me.

Kill me. Kill me. I don't want to be here.

The second guy pulls the man off me. I can hear him zipping his pants back up, and they rush out of the room. Laying there, hyperventilating, trying to catch my breath, I only wish he could have succeeded and helped me to take my last breath.

Should I try to tell someone or just lay here until tomorrow? I don't know who I can trust. The smell of cologne lines my sheets. Throwing them on the ground, I get up and put on a second layer of clothes. Tonight will just be an extra cold night. Who would try to do such a thing? It has to be staff members because who has access to the rooms this late at night? I look at the clock—2:47. Ms. Charlie is usually on duty, and I know she would never. She's trans, but would she assist and let someone else attempt to come in and rape me?

She doesn't seem like she's that type of person. I think I can trust Ms. Charlie. Maybe they came in while she was on a smoke or lunch break. It's probably best that I wait until tomorrow and discuss it with Rosa. She can help me.

Reaching over, I take my notebook and pen out of the nightstand and begin writing.

Sorrowful spirits watching my moves,

Clinging to my presence as if my life makes sense,

Following me throughout my home and watching my every move,

Telling me life has more and my potential is not yet reached.

Sorrowful spirits hum in my ears, saying it's up to me to breathe the air they no longer need, eat the food they no longer taste, to feed on love because they no longer can.

Sorrowful spirits taunt me at times. Threatening my dreams with silly nightmares. While whispering in my ears, "Wake up."

And I awaken and decide not to sleep. Awake I lay at the bewitching hour,

Watching the spirits enter my room, they prance around, watching me watch them.

So sad they look, but they wipe my tears. They are the ones no longer breathing.

They are the ones hiding in the shadows.

But yet, their sorrow is for me.

Dropping the pen, sleep once again sets sail, conquering my mind.

As I begin to dream, emotions soar, and rage twists my soul, and for once, I know for a fact that this is a dream, a distant dream, yet this dream connects to my heart and sours my being. The orange and red colors surrounding me are so vivid. My skin heats up as the flames grow to the ceiling. Sweat runs down my temples. Fear surfaces in my heart and circulates my veins. The smell of gasoline rummages through the air.

Run, my mind screams, but my body stands there, observing. Admiring the colors spread about, watching the two still bodies lay on the floor covered in blood.

I turn my head to the side, intrigued by their lack of motion. Together they lay there, eyes still open, peaceful faces. Lovers finally able to be together in peace. I'm happy for them; my soul rejoices for their new journey.

Looking away from the bodies, I look in a mirror that stands in front of me, and behind me stands a tall, dark shadow. It stares at me, and I can feel the pain and suffering radiating from its vibrations. The fear in my heart intensifies, and finally, my mind says to run, so I run, bumping into tables, knocking over a plant. I dash from the den to the kitchen and to the front door.

My ankle aches from being inactive for so long, but I shake it off and continue to run to my car. Digging in the pockets of my jeans, my finger hits every corner of the cloth until I'm able to grip the keys and pull them out. Pushing the button to unlock the car, I jump in, immediately locking the doors.

Looking in my rearview mirror, I can see the shadow standing at the front of the house, watching me as it walks down the porch steps. I turn the ignition on, put the car in drive, and begin backing up out of the drive way. When I arrive at the street, I immediately put the car in drive and push my foot all the way down on the pedal. My heart thumps in my chest, my breathing rough and heavy. My Honda accelerates slowly, and tears gather in my eyes, fear surrounding and encaging me. I finally break down, uncontrollably crying. The car changes gears and speeds up rapidly. Curiosity gets the best of me, and I look in my rearview mirror. The flames are enormous, so I turn back and continue to drive.

Footsteps wake me from my sleep.

"Summer, it's breakfast time. Are you going?" Rosa asks as she stands in the doorway. The sunlight illuminates the room, blinding me when I open my eyes. A dream so vivid, could it have been a memory? Am I a murderer? Did I truly kill them?

"Rosa, something happened last night..."

"What happened, chica?"

"Someone came into my room and attacked me. I think they were going to try to rape me."

"What!" Rosa exclaims.

"Did you see who it was?"

"No, it was in the middle of the night, and there was only a little light coming in from the window, so I couldn't make out who it was."

"I don't know how that's possible. Charlie was at the station last night. Did you talk to her?"

Most of the staff members refer to Ms. Charlie as Charlie.

"Rosa, I was so scared. I was unsure what to do. I feel like I can trust you, and I knew you would be here this morning, so I decided to wait."

"Are you sure? Could you have dreamed it?"

"Rosa, someone came into my room!"

"Stay in here, and let me call Dr. Mocker."

Rosa slips out of the room, leaving me with a flicker of hope that the surveillance cameras would reveal the intruder's identity, presumably one of the staff members. Pushing myself up from the bed, I ease my slippers on and go into the bathroom to take a shower. The faint trace of cologne still hangs in the air, a persistent reminder of their presence. A sniff at my shirt, which confirms that the scent had clung to my clothes. Hastily, I yank the shirt over my head and quickly step in the shower, turn the water on and step beneath the shower's head. The water initially sends a shiver down my spine, but soon, a warm, comforting embrace envelopes my body. I lather my towel with soap, scrubbing my skin with force determined to get rid of the lingering cologne. In the soothing cascade of water, a distant noise filters through the bathroom door. It has to be Rosa returning. Hurriedly, I rinse off, dry myself, and slip into fresh, clean clothes.

"Summer," Rosa's voice calls from beyond the bathroom door.

"I'm coming," I respond, exiting the bathroom.

"Dr. Mocker needs to see you right away," she informs me.

"All right, I'm ready," I reply, falling into step beside her. Together, we walked down the hallway, which appeared oddly deserted. Everyone must be breakfast.

"The security cameras should be able to identify who entered my room, shouldn't they?" I inquired, seeking reassurance.

"Yes, they should," Rosa assures me, her voice conveying hope.

"Stop for a second," says Rosa.

We stop in the hall, and she stares at my face, then gently rubs her finger on the top of my cheek under my left eye.

"Ouch!" I exclaim.

"You have a bruise here," she tells me, and we continue to walk down the hall.

We approach Dr. Mocker's door, and Rosa lightly knocks.

"Come in," he calls.

We walk in, and he's sitting at his massive desk. His glasses are pushed up close to his nose, and his hands are clasped together against his chin.

"Summer, have a seat, and please tell me what happened. Rosa, stay in here as a witness."

I tell them everything from when I awoke last night to when they left my room.

"Do you, by any chance, know about what time it was that this occurred?"

"Two-forty-seven AM. I remember looking at the clock when it was over."

Dr. Mocker picks up his phone and dials a number. "Jason, I need you to immediately send me all video footage from the third floor east wing last night between two and three AM."

He hangs up the phone and says, "We will know who came into your room in a few minutes."

Dr. Mocker turns his computer on and begins pushing buttons.

"Dr. Mocker, I don't know if you noticed, but Summer has a bruise on her face, too," says Rosa.

He gets up and walks toward me. He lifts my chin with his finger and examines my face from side to side.

"This is unacceptable!" he exclaims while walking back to his desk. He looks at the computer again, shaking his head. The phone rings, and he picks it up.

"What do you mean no footage?!" He slams the phone on the receiver and looks my way.

"Apparently, the storm knocked the electricity out, and there is no footage of who was in the hall."

"This is a hospital. It doesn't have a generator?" I ask him, astonished.

"Yes, it does, but it didn't power them." Dr. Mocker picks up his phone again. "Get Charlie Grant on the line ASAP."

He hangs up the phone and looks toward Rosa and me. "I'm going to get to the bottom of this. Are you sure more didn't happen than what you're telling me?"

"Yes, I am."

"Dr. Mocker, Summer hasn't eaten breakfast. How about I take her to the cafeteria?"

"Yes, do that. Summer, can you step outside the door a moment?"

"Sure," I tell him.

I get up, walk outside the office, and close the door behind me. Curiosity erupts in me like a volcano. What is it he doesn't want me to hear? I get as close as possible to the door and listen.

My ears struggle but catch the words, "Don't tell anyone about this. I don't want it to get out. The media would be all over it. Let's keep it in-house. I'll deal with whoever did it," Dr. Mocker says very softly.

"Yes, sir," Rosa responds.

I hear footsteps approaching the door, and I quickly move away and pretend to be looking out a window.

"You ready?" Rosa says as she approaches me.

"Yes."

We begin walking toward the cafeteria.

"You don't have to walk with me," I tell her.

"Well, let me at least walk with you to the cafeteria doors, and then I'll meet you back there, and we can go back to Dr. Mocker's office together."

"Okay."

I think about what my conversation is going to be like with Whitney and Eric. I bet they have an idea of who came into my room.

"Maybe you shouldn't talk about what happened last night. We don't want to scare anyone," Rosa tells me.

I stop walking. "What? Are you guys trying to cover this up?"

"No, no, no, not at all. I just don't want anyone to be afraid."

"What about me being afraid? What if they come back?"

"Summer, I promise you're safe. Dr. Mocker is going to take care of this."

"Can I just walk the rest of the way alone, please? Or am I on lockdown, even though I was the one that was attacked?"

"No, go ahead, but at least let me meet you back here so we can walk back to Dr. Mocker's office together."

I briskly walk away. Tears accumulate in my eyes. I really don't understand what's going on on this place.

Quickly, I wipe my tears and take a deep breath to walk into the cafeteria. Scanning the room for Eric and Whitney, I don't see either one. I go to the cereal bar, get some cornflakes and a banana, and then I begin looking for a place to sit where I can be alone.

"Summer? Summer?"

I hear Whitney calling my name. I turn, and she's sitting by herself. Instantaneously, I go to her table.

"I'm so happy to see you," I tell her.

"What's wrong? Are you okay?"

I tell Whitney everything, including the interaction I just had with Rosa. She listens without any interruptions.

"I don't trust them! I don't trust this place. So many things just don't add up. You can't get that ECT," says Whitney.

"Where's Eric? Maybe he can talk to his dad. Maybe his dad can help me."

"I haven't seen Eric today."

I look across the room, and I can see Rosa standing in the doorway of the cafeteria.

"Look, Rosa is watching me now," I tell Whitney.

"Pretend not to notice and just eat your food."

Whitney takes a bite out of a jellied biscuit, and I eat a spoonful of my cereal, then peel my banana and use my spoon to put pieces in my cereal.

"I really want to remember more. Can you come to my room tonight?"

"I'll try if Ms. Charlie is working tonight."

We continue to eat our breakfast. Every few minutes, I look over toward the door and see Rosa watching us. Paula, the Brunswick Bully, walks up to our table.

"I see you guys got someone watching ya'll."

I look at her and don't reply. She sets her tray down and takes a seat.

"Hey, Whitney," she says.

"I'm going to go ahead and get this over with," I tell Whitney as I get up from the table and start walking to put my tray away.

"Leaving so soon?" Paula asks me.

Pretending like I don't hear her, I continue to walk. She's pure evil; the way she treated me previously was hideous. My words for her are minimal, if any at all. Taking my time walking over to Rosa, I no longer feel like I can trust her. I'm the victim but being treated like the suspect.

"How was your breakfast?" she asks me.

"Okay," I reply.

We begin walking toward Dr. Mocker's office. She smiles at me as if everything is normal. Maybe everything is normal for her, but this is the twilight zone for me. So much has occurred this past week. My mind spins in confusion, and if I get the ECT, that's only going to make matters worse. I need to convince Dr. Mocker that I don't need it. My thoughts seem logical to me. I don't feel I've been irrational or violent in any way. All of my actions have been compliant. To me, it doesn't seem like I'm a true candidate for ECT. In addition, I was attacked by someone here—that should give me some leverage.

We arrive at Dr. Mocker's office. Rosa knocks on the door and then walks in. He's sitting in his chair, looking at papers. He looks at us with a straight face, with no lines, dimples, or creases. But two small bags lie under each eye; I didn't notice them before. He raises a cup of coffee to his lips and takes a few sips.

"You guys are back."

"Did you find out anything?" Rosa asks.

"Well, apparently, Charlie had an upset stomach last night and was in and out of the bathroom throughout the night. She did not notice anything suspicious. I have security checking to see who scanned their keycards around that time. We will get to the bottom of this. Rosa, you can go back to the station. I'm going to keep Summer here to talk."

"Okay, Dr. Mocker," Rosa says as she walks to the door and leaves.

"Have a seat."

I sit down in a chair in front of the doctor's desk.

"I'm truly sorry this happened to you. This is a very secure facility. One thing is for certain, we're going to find out what happened. Are there any extra details that you remember?"

"In all honesty, it happened so fast. I was so scared."

"We could move you to a different room again? You could share a room with someone, or we have a room right across from the nurse's station that we can put you in?"

"I'll take the room across from the nurse's station."

"With so much going on, how are you feeling?"

Everything feels like a nightmare. I want to scream, punch, kick, hit, and tear the walls down. You're so handsome to me, and I want to jump your bones. I miss my husband, whom I killed, and nights at this place are like being in a never-ending horror story where I can't outrun the killer.

These thoughts bolt through my mind like lightning, but my response to the doctor is only, "I feel okay. I've been wondering if there's any way we can skip the ECT session? I've been through so much and am just not ready for it."

"Summer, I've been observing you, and it doesn't seem like you're taking your medication, or maybe the medication isn't working. You need the ECT session."

"Dr. Mocker, why do I need the session? I'm not violent. I'm compliant."

"You're a manic depressant, and I don't want to see you spiral down. I've watched you do it before, and it's not good. You become delusional, thinking your dead husband is out to get you. We've been working so hard to get you on the right path, and I want to stay consistent with the treatments."

"I would like to return to my room now."

Dr. Mocker looks at me for a few seconds. He pushes his glasses up and leans back. Then he rubs his hands together.

"I tell you what. I'll put the ECT off for two days."

Two whole days!

"Okay, thank you, Dr. Mocker. Can I go to my room now?"

"Sure, I'll let you know if I find anything else out about last night."

Getting up from the chair, I can feel the lust I have for Dr. Mocker slowly oozing out. My heart feels heavy as I walk out of his office as if there is much more to say and discuss. I still don't understand this ECT stuff, and I don't want to understand it. I just want it to be completely over and behind me. Walking down the hall, I see Eric.

"Eric!" I yell.

He keeps walking. I speed up to catch up with him.

"Eric!" I yell again.

He continues to walk as if he doesn't hear my loud shouts.

I go into a brisk run and catch up with him.

"Hey, Eric!"

"I thought I heard someone say my name."

"I was looking for you at breakfast. Where were you?"

"I overslept and didn't go to breakfast, but I'll definitely be at lunch," he tells me.

"Of course," I say with a laugh.

"I'm sorry, Summer."

"For not going to breakfast?" I burst into laughter.

"No, Summer. I'm sorry for last night."

Eric and I both stop in our tracks. I look at him and see a long scratch across his cheek.

"You bastard!" I scream.

"I'm sorry. I'm really sorry."

Time disappears, everything in front of me temporarily vanishes, and when it comes back, I'm swinging and kicking at Eric while he shields his face from my blows.

"We were supposed to be friends, you asshole! How could you? You piece of shit," rings from my mouth.

I can feel someone holding me, but it doesn't stop my kicking. Finally, it registers we're surrounded by four or five people in white trying to stop me. The sting of a needle enters my arm, and I also begin fighting the staff. Whoever touches me gets a blow. Eric somehow disappears from sight. Breathing in quick, heavy breaths, my adrenaline surges as Carl tries to hold me. My nostrils breathe in the scent of Carl's cologne, and it's the same scent I smelled last night and this morning. This bastard was in on it, too. My adrenaline pumps harder, but my strength begins to leave my body. My limbs become limp.

I see Dr. Mocker staring at me from the corner of my eyes. I see patients and staff doing the same. I fall to my knees. Carl and a security guard who I've never seen before picks me up. Rosa pushes a wheelchair toward us. They put me in it and began pushing me away. Looking up at Carl, I want to tell him I know. I want to spit on him and kick him in the balls. I will myself to stand. Please stand up, Summer, but I don't stand. My body just sits there, disobeying my order. Whatever is in that needle is some strong stuff.

It has never occurred to me how long the halls are or how many doors line the corridor. Rosa's keycard is clipped right on the tail of her shirt. I bet it would be easy to steal it. I wonder what's it like to glide down a rainbow. When will this ride be over? I'm tired. My eyelids and lashes battle me. I try to keep them open, but they keep falling down. The war is over, and I let them win. My eyes shut; I relax and enjoy the ride.

We reach my room, and they transfer me from the wheelchair to the bed.

"Rosa, it's him," I whisper to her.

My whisper goes unanswered. Everyone leaves the room. Lying in bed, my body is too limp to take any actions of any kind. Swiftly, I doze off.

REMEMBERING

"**W**ake up, Summer. Wake up." I slowly awaken to Whitney and Ms. Charlie standing over me. My eyes open and fall back.

"She has been asleep for over eight hours. The drugs should have worn off by now," I hear Ms. Charlie telling Whitney.

"Summer. Summer?" She calls out my name.

I open my eyes again, and this time, they stay open. Looking up at the clock, I see that the time is 12:47. I've been asleep a long time.

"How do you feel?" Whitney asks.

"Eric and Carl came in here last night. Eric tried to rape me." Ms. Charlie puts her hand over her mouth.

"Summer, I talked to Eric, and he told me to give you this."

Whitney hands me a folded piece of paper. I get it and throw it on the floor.

"I need to alert security and inform them of Carl's actions," says Ms. Charlie.

"Wait, Ms. Charlie, can you please give me and Whitney fifteen minutes alone?"

"Yes, sure. But Whitney will have to return to her room before I call them," says Ms. Charlie as she turns to walk out the door.

"I can't believe those assholes," Ms. Charlie says under her breath.

"Are you sure you want to do this? You're not too tired?" Whitney asks me.

"I'm fine."

"Try to relax. You have to be relaxed," Whitney says as she rubs the sides of my face. She places one of her hands on my heart.

"Marie is here with us. Tell her what you want."

"I want to know what happened to me. Please, help me."

"She says she has already shown you what happened in your dreams."

"So I killed them?"

Whitney stares at the corner of the room. I look in the direction she stares and see a bright white light moving toward us. The light is in the shape of a person, and the closer it gets, the more identifiable it becomes. The figure is a woman. She stands in front of us and places her hand on my forehead. Instantaneously, I'm no longer in the hospital room but in a room in my house, hiding in a closet with my physical past self.

Although it's dark, I see myself crouched down, peeking out of the closet. Yelling and screaming swarm the air, floating in from the other room. I look out the door and see Charles and Christina sitting on my gray leather sectional, staring up at someone. From my angle, I can't quite make out the person. Remembering from my last experience that I'm not visible, I walk out of the closet, leaving my past self peeking out.

"You've been sleeping with my wife all this time?!" says the man standing over them, whose voice begins to sound familiar.

"I'm so sorry. I truly am," says Christina.

"We have been working together, spending a lot of time together, and it just happened," says Charles.

"How would you like it if I slept with your wife?" says the male voice.

The voice finally registers—it's Dr. Mocker! Shock spins my thoughts. It truly is Dr. Mocker. I move to the side of him where I can see the front of him, and yes, it's the doctor, and he's holding a giant machete. A gun sticks out the front of his pants. Now I see why they are sitting on the couch, not getting up while he stands over them.

"Edwin, Christina says y'all's relationship has been over for years now. She says you've been cheating with someone you work with."

"I've seen text messages from a Delisa from your job," Christina says.

My hand covers my mouth. Delisa and Dr. Mocker! Tears roll down my face. Everyone that I trusted has betrayed me!

"She's no one. I love you, Christina. You're my wife, who I want to be with," says Dr. Mocker.

"Edwin, she's pregnant, and we've decided to be together."

Dr. Mocker quickly raises the hand holding the machete and, with quickness, brings it across Charles' throat. Blood sprays out, covering the doctor and Christina. Christina screams, and it drowns out my scream from the closet. My heart drops, and my hands grip my face. Christina stands up, and the doctor swiftly approaches her and sticks the knife in her abdomen. He pulls it out and repeats it over and over again.

I run to the door and remember that I'm only here in spirit; I must continue to watch this gruesome act if I want to know everything. Christina's body lies on the sectional, and the doctor keeps stabbing her lifeless corpse. Blood sprays in the air. He stops, grabs Charles' body, and pulls it to the floor. He then kicks Charles in the head, gets on his knees, and stabs Charles multiple times. Nausea churns my stomach. Dr. Mocker gets up and pulls Christina's body over to Charles. He takes his shirt and pants off and throws them on the floor. He stands there in only a T-shirt and basketball shorts that he must have worn under his clothes. Then he walks away. I look over at the closet, wondering when I'm going to run out for help.

The door doesn't open.

The doctor returns, carrying a big red gasoline container. He covers the bodies and his clothes in gas, lights a match, and walks out of the room. The flames race over the bodies, covering every inch. It then catches on the carpet, moving to the sectional and the curtains behind it. Finally, I see myself slowly walking out of the closet and standing over the bodies, watching, half-smiling. Who is this person I'm watching? The look on my face looks like I'm enjoying this scene. I see myself looking up, and Dr. Mocker has returned.

I see the other me run outside, down the steps, and into the car. I slide into the backseat and ride, wondering what my next move will be. We move down the driveway until we reach the main street. I look back to see Dr. Mocker getting into his car and riding behind us. I watch myself speed down the street, not stopping at any stop signs, darting through traffic. Tears cover my flesh, and my arms shake while my hands grip the steering wheel. After we turn a few corners, I look back and don't see Dr. Mocker's white Range Rover, but I'm still driving like a bat out of hell.

We approach a cemetery, and I recognize it as St. Louis Cemetery. A drizzle of rain falls from the sky. Homeless people with tents laid out along the sidewalk, and one man stands about, leaning on a light pole. He looks like he's selling drugs. I follow myself as I get out of the car and walk to the cemetery. I can tell my past self is overlooking all the homeless people and must be focused on my destination, Marie's grave. I remember the doctor said they found me here. The sound of a gun pierces through the air. Not turning back, I see myself rushing to Marie's tomb.

"Get back here, bitch," seeps into my ear. A door slams, and I'm suddenly back in the hospital room, sitting with Whitney, and now Ms. Charlie stands in the room again.

"Dr. Mocker killed my husband!"

"What? That sounds crazy," says Ms. Charlie.

"I believe you, Whitney says as she wraps her arms around me.

"Are you sure Eric and Carl came in here last night? Summer, you have been on some heavy drugs, and what if all of this is in your head?" asks Ms. Charlie.

"He did it," I whisper to Whitney.

"Come on, Whitney. Let's get you back to your room because I don't want any trouble! I got bills to pay. I need my job. I don't want to report something that might be a delusion."

Whitney lets go of me, stands up, and begins walking out of the room with Ms. Charlie.

"I'll see you tomorrow," she tells me.

The door creaks closed behind them. Sitting on the edge of my bed, looking down, I spot the piece of paper Eric gave Whitney to give to me. I pick it up and unfold it. The paper is similar to the paper in the notebook Dr. Mocker gave me.

I'm sorry,
I was promised I would get out in two weeks
if I went to your room and scared you.
I wasn't going to rape you or hurt you.
It was just to scare you. I'm sorry.

I folded the letter back up and walked over to my bedroom door. Forgetting it was locked, I pulled on the handle, and, of course, it didn't open. Let me relax before talking to Ms. Charlie. I don't want to sound hysterical. I've got to convince them I'm not crazy.

I make myself look more presentable by strengthening my clothes, taking my ponytail, and redoing it. Then, I lightly knock on the door. It clicks, and I step out and walk up to the station where Ms. Charlie is standing, looking in my direction.

"Is everything okay?" she asks me.

"Look at this letter I received from Eric."

She takes the letter from my hand, unfolds it, and reads it.

"Well, this is proof it happened, and it was him."

"This bruise on the side of my face is also proof."

Ms. Charlie looks at my face.

"Dr. Mocker and Delisa been having an affair," explodes out of my mouth.

"How do you know this? You can say whatever you want, but without proof, it doesn't mean anything. I'm not saying I don't believe you, but many people here are delusional. They see things, hear things, and think they have powers and can fly. People here are crazy, and it's not any offense to you, but you'll have to prove whatever you say."

"Can I, please, use your computer?"

"No, it's cameras around here, but go to your room. I'll get my phone out of my locker, and you can use my phone."

"Thank you, thank you, thank you."

"Hurry up and go before I change my mind."

"I can't believe I'm helping a crazy person," Ms. Charlie whispers to herself.

I briskly walk back to the room to wait for Ms. Charlie. It's like ants are crawling all over my skin. My nerves are exploding in my body. If I can prove the connection between me, my husband, Dr. Mocker, and his wife, then people have to believe me.

Ms. Charlie walks in carrying her phone, unlocks it, and hands it to me.

"You have five minutes."

Five minutes should be plenty of time to research the fire. I put 'Charles James' in the search engine, but nothing comes up. I try house fire in Timber Ridge,' and an article comes up with the title 'Two Dead in House Fire in Timber Ridge.' Scanning the article, I hit the jackpot. Quickly, I read it, looking for the names of the people involved. No names listed; two dead, arson, awaiting autopsy, but no names of the victim or suspect. Moving on to a different article, I quickly read it, but it doesn't list any names either. Finally, I decide to try a different approach.

Ms. Charlie stands with her body halfway through the door.

"Do you have any social media accounts?" I ask her.

"Yes, why?"

"Can you look up Christina Mocker?"

I hand her the phone, and she begins pressing the buttons.

"Is this her?" she says as she turns the phone toward me and lets me examine the picture.

"Yes! That's her. Now, can you look up my husband's page, Charles James, and look for a picture in December of me, her, and a man? We took that picture together at the Christmas party last year."

We sit in silence while she works her phone, looking for the picture.

"I see it," she says, with a small burst of excitement in her voice.

"My husband and Dr. Mocker's wife were having an affair, and she got pregnant. Dr. Mocker found out and killed them both. I don't think there was enough evidence to convict me, so, according to him, I tried to commit suicide multiple times while in jail awaiting trial, so they put me in here. He's trying to keep me drugged and give me ECT, so I don't remember seeing him do it."

"Dr. Mocker runs this place, so I don't think we will get anywhere talking to anyone here. I have a cousin who works for the police department. Let me talk to him tomorrow and find out what can be done."

These words enter my ears, and I'm hugging Ms. Charlie before I know it. That's the best thing I have heard in a while.

"Thank you," I tell her as I squeeze her. She looks up at the clock on the wall.

"I'm supposed to be giving you medicine tonight. I'll bring them to you, but what you do with them is your business."

"Thanks, Ms. Charlie." She leaves the room, and I take a hot shower, washing away yesterday's hurt, pain, and sadness. Getting dressed, relief showers over me, and I look forward to what tomorrow brings.

MORNING

orning comes with swiftness. I think I still have some of the drugs from yesterday in my system because I slept like a baby. No crazy dreams, no disturbances, just plain ole' good, deep, rejuvenating sleep. Getting up from bed and standing in front of the window, I bathe in the warm, soothing sun rays. They bring so much comfort to my being. Stepping into the bathroom, I shower quickly, brush my teeth, and put on clean, fresh clothes.

Ms. Charlie has already left, and Maria is now on duty. Hopefully, I'll meet with Dr. Mocker today, especially since yesterday's incident. He usually meets patients after incidents. How should I confront him? How will he react once he knows I know? He can't outright hurt me because he won't be able to explain it. I grab my notebook and begin writing. Carefully, I tear the page out of my notebook, proofread it again, sign it, fold it in half twice, and stuff it into my pocket. A brief knock on my door, and Maria steps in.

"I got you breakfast."

"So am I on lockdown? I can't go to the cafeteria?"

"Dr. Mocker has to authorize it. What happened yesterday?"

"It was Eric and Carl that came into my room the other night."

Maria quickly puts the tray down. "I did hear you thought someone came into your room," she says.

"Thought! I know someone came into my room. Look at this bruise on my cheek and the scratch on Eric's face."

She looks at my cheek.

"I do see a light bruise. What exactly happened?"

I tell her about Eric and Carl coming to my room, and then I tell her about when I saw Eric and the scratch on his cheek, and I lost control.

"Eat your breakfast, and let me notify Dr. Mocker. I'll be back after talking to him."

She leaves the room. If only she knew Dr. Mocker is a psychopathic killer who set me up for murder. Glancing over at the food tray, my nose turns up; my appetite is nonexistent. Food is the absolute last thing on my mind. I must figure out how to confront Dr. Mocker. He has all the power. Almost every time I enter his room, he's always sipping on coffee. Taking the pills I've been hiding out of my drawer and using my tray of food to crush the pills, I think about how I can maybe put them in his coffee. I would have to talk to him for at least thirty to forty-five minutes for the pills to take effect, and then I could steal his keycard from his desk and try to leave this facility.

Maria walks back into the room.

"I just found out Eric was released this morning."

"What? That's crazy!" burst out of my mouth.

I want to tell her about the apology note he wrote, but then she might ask how I got it, and I don't want to get Ms. Charlie in any trouble. Plus, I don't even have the note. Ms. Charlie kept it.

"I told Dr. Mocker what you said about Eric, but I'm unsure how he will handle it. He says you can meet with him after breakfast."

"I'm not going to eat breakfast, so you might as well just take me now."

Getting up and walking toward Maria, she picks up my food tray, and we walk toward the nurse's station. Maria stops at the station and sets the tray down, then she picks up the phone and makes a call.

"Hello, Dr. Mocker. Summer is ready to come to your office now." Maria pauses for a few seconds and then says, "Okay, we're on our way." She looks at me and says, "We can go now."

We begin walking toward the doctor's office. My palms and underarms start to sweat profusely. The sound of my heartbeat thumps in my ears, and it feels like it's playing hot scotch under my skin. My breathing slows, and it's as if I've forgotten how to breathe. I stop momentarily and sit in one of the wicker chairs that line the hallway.

Maria stops, looks, and walks over to me.

"Are you okay?"

"I just need a minute," I say as I begin hyperventilating. "But I'm okay," I tell her while holding my chest.

She grabs my wrist, holds it, and looks at the watch on her arm. My heartbeat slowly decreases, and my breath returns. However, fear keeps exploding in my joints, muscles, and nerves, coming out of my body in a rapid sweat.

"I think you're just having an anxiety attack. Stay here. I'm going to get you a wheelchair," Maria says, quickly walking away. Warm teardrops roll down my face. I try to stop them, thinking happy thoughts. Hopefully, I'll be seeing Angelique soon. I'll be home—well, maybe not home since my house was burned down by this doctor that

I'm about to see. More tears violently surface. An abominable ache bounces around in my body, stretching my mind and pulling at my soul. I don't think I can go in there. I jump up out of the chair and start pacing the floor.

"Summer?"

I look up and see Whitney. Quickly, I run to and hug her. Her compassionate embrace gives me a minute's release, and the tears gradually slow down.

"It's going to be okay," she tells me.

"I'm on my way to Dr. Mocker's office now," I whisper in her ear while slowly taking the note out of my pocket and sliding it into hers. She rubs her hand up and down my back.

"Ms. Charlie says she's going to help you, and I believe her," she tells me.

"I'm afraid to face Dr. Mocker now that I know."

We drop our embrace, and I walk back to the wicker chair to sit back down.

"Let Marie give you strength."

"This is too much," I tell her.

"Ladies, you can't hang out in the hallway," says a security guard.

Looking up, I see a tall guy standing above me.

"I'm waiting for Maria. She went to get me a wheelchair because I'm not feeling well."

"And you?" he says, pointing to Whitney.

"Coming from breakfast. I'll see you later, Summer," Whitney says as she walks away.

"I guess I'll wait here with you until Maria returns."

"I guess you will." Asshole.

My breathing and heartbeat finally slows to normal.

"Is everything okay?" Maria asks as she walks up.

"Yes, I was just waiting with her until you returned," says the guard.

"Thank you," Maria tells him.

I get up from the chair and sit down in the wheelchair. Maria starts pushing me down the hall. Each time before, I enjoyed going to Dr. Mocker's office. I had a teenage crush on him. The thought of liking him now stirs my stomach and makes me want to vomit. The dream that we slept together repulses me. How did I not see the evil in him sooner? We approach his office. The door sends shivers up and down my spine. A few tears make their way down my cheek. I wipe them quickly; I don't want him to see my torment. Taking a deep breath in, blowing out anxiety, my legs shake uncontrollably. This is the man who murdered my husband, his wife, and her unborn baby. Maria knocks on the door.

"You can come in." His voice stunts my breath.

Breathe, breathe, breathe. Slowly, it comes again.

Maria pushes me through the door right beside the doctor's desk. Our glances meet, and I rapidly look away.

"Maria, I'll call you when I'm ready for you to come and get her." Maria nods and exits the room.

Dr. Mocker's eyebrows go together, and he looks me up and down.

"Are you okay?" he asks.

Words roll around but don't quite surface. I just nod.

He puts his hands together and leans back in his leather chair. He has coffee sitting on his desk—if I can somehow get the pills in his cup...

"You seem nervous."

"Eric and Carl are the ones that assaulted me."

He sits back up in his chair. "Is that all that's wrong?"

"Isn't that enough?"

Dr. Mocker gets up from his chair, walks around his desk, and leans on the front of it directly in front of me. My foot taps against the metal of the wheelchair. The doctor places his hand on my leg.

"It's okay. You don't have to be so nervous."

He knows I remember. I can feel it. Someone knocks on the door.

"Yes?" says the doctor.

Delisa walks in. "Can I see u for a second?"

Dr. Mocker walks over and stands in the doorway, facing outward. I can hear whispers. Swiftly, I jump up, pull the smashed-up pills out of my pocket, reach over his desk, and pour them into the cup of coffee. The white powder floats on the top. Briskly, I sit back down in my chair. I've got to stir it. Getting back up from my seat, I look over my shoulder to ensure his back is to me. I pick up a pen off his desk, stir the coffee, and expeditiously sit back down. My palms shine from the sweat. The door closes, and the doctor walks back over to me.

"I'm sorry about that. There was an incident with another patient."

"It's okay."

"Are you hot? You're sweating."

"Yes, it's a little hot in here."

Dr. Mocker walks over and adjusts the thermostat.

"Carl will be fired," he tells me.

"That's good."

Memories flash in my mind of Dr. Mocker, covered in blood, stabbing the dead bodies repeatedly, blood spilling and spraying out, pieces of flesh and clothing flying in the air as he pulled the machete out. His frowning face was staring down at them, his arm had moved ferociously. Tears flowed down his face, yet it didn't stop his savage actions and the look he gave me when he saw I was standing there. He wanted to kill me, too. I can't look him in the eyes right now. If I make eye contact with him, all the pain and hurt of what I saw is going to come out of me.

"You don't seem like yourself today," he tells me.

I stare down at the floor. "I'm still shaken up from yesterday," I tell him, not taking my eyes off the dark cherry, ashy hardwood floors.

"Maybe I need to increase your medication again?"

"I don't think that's necessary. The medicine already keeps me extremely drowsy to the point that it's hard for me to think clearly."

Dr. Mocker walks over to his desk, opens a locked drawer, and pulls out a bottle of brandy.

"How about we have a drink?"

He pours two drinks, pushing a glass over to me. He drinks his glass and pours another before my mind can fully register what's happening.

"Summer, let's cut the chit-chat. You remember what happened, don't you?"

"You killed them. I watched you for what seemed like an eternity stab their flesh. What you did was sick, yet I'm the one in here!" I yell at the doctor.

"I saw the look you had on your face when you were standing over their bodies. You were happy! I bet you didn't know he was planning on leaving you," he says calmly and serenely.

He's right, for a split second. I was happy when I first stood over their dead bodies. They lay there together, and the thought of him leaving me was stuck in my mind, but when reality kicked in and I realized it was real and couldn't be taken back, I was disgusted. He took two people's lives. Regardless of what they did and were doing, they didn't deserve to die. From the expression on his face right now, he has no regrets.

"I don't wish death on anyone!" I tell the doctor.

"So, why were you smiling?" he asks, staring me in the eyes. I stare back. I'm beyond words. This is a murderer staring me in the face.

"You should not have run. I wasn't going to hurt you," he tells me.

"Then why am I in here?"

Dr. Mocker takes a seat in his chair. "Once you ran to the cemetery, I followed you and found you lying on the ground beside a grave. I think someone tried to rob you because you were bleeding from your head, and you were unresponsive. I called the police, and they came and took you away in an ambulance. The next day, I saw on the news that they were charging you with the murders. I knew they didn't have any real evidence, but a neighbor said she saw you driving off very fast around the time of the fire. I guess when you woke up, and they told you about the fire and your husband, you tried to kill yourself. The prosecutor must have realized it would be hard to get a conviction, but because you tried to kill yourself, he persuaded the judge to order you to be placed here. In a nutshell, that's what happened," Dr. Mocker says as he folds his arms and leans back in his chair like he's some type of superior king.

"What about the ECT?" I ask him.

"Do you really think I would let you turn me in?"

"You could have killed me at the cemetery. Why didn't you?"

"I'm not a murderer, and you endured the same pain as me. I did us both a favor when I killed them," he tells me.

"I loved my husband." Tears stir in my eyes, but I try my hardest to hold them back.

"And I loved my wife," he says. "And if you loved your husband so much, why have you been flirting with me and writing about me in the notebook I gave you?"

"How do you know what I wrote?"

"Why do you think I gave you the book?" he asks me.

"So, where do we go from here?"

"You'll be going to get ECT. That's where you'll be going."

"I'll tell everyone in here."

"You can try, but you'll not even remember this conversation in the next few hours."

"Please, Dr. Mocker. Please don't."

"You have given me no choice. I'm sorry."

"Can I at least have a few drinks, please?" I ask him, trying to buy time so I can figure out what to do next. I pick up the small glass he had pushed my way and take a big gulp of the brandy. It runs down my throat, burning my esophagus and my chest.

"Whew," comes from my mouth as I frown. It's strong liquor. The doctor watches me and takes a sip of his coffee.

"So, did you have Eric and Carl scare me that night?"

"I knew it would fuel you to make a scene."

"And Delisa pretending I choked her was to make me look crazy, too?"

"You seem to be up to speed, and that's why you need the ECT."

"What if I don't tell anyone? Just let me out of here. Let me be free. I won't tell," I plead with Dr. Mocker.

"Summer, I can't trust you."

He picks up his coffee and takes another sip.

"You can trust me! Really, I think we should be together, anyway. I've had a crush on you since our first session, and it seems you feel some type of way about me, too." His arrogance kicks in, and I can tell he's intrigued by what I'm saying.

"Can I pour myself another glass?" I ask him in my softest voice.

"Be my guest."

Dr. Mocker gets up from his chair and walks over to me. He takes my ponytail down and runs his fingers through my hair. I take a sip of the brandy, then stand up, facing the doctor. We look each other in the eyes. His eyes are mystifying. I kiss him, and he kisses me back. He picks me up and sits me on his desk. Gently, he kisses my neck and nibbles on my ear. He lifts my shirt and rubs my breast.

I can sense the palpable tension in the room as his hardness presses against my pants, sending shivers down my spine. My body reacts instinctively, my core throbbing with a mixture of fear and adrenaline. Desperation drives me to reach for the heavy, round bottle of brandy nearby. My trembling fingers clasp around its neck, and I clench it with every ounce of strength I possess.

Summoning every reserve of determination, I muster the energy to forcefully push the doctor away. With a sudden burst of might, I bring the unforgiving weight of the brandy bottle down upon him, smashing it against his skull. A sickening thud reverberates through the room as blood begins to trickle from the wound, staining his white shirt.

He stumbles back, his equilibrium shattered, and his vision seems blurred. The doctor manages a few faltering steps toward me, a sinister glint in his eyes. But then, as if defeated by the gravity of his injuries, he collapses to the floor, his body limp and lifeless.

For a breathless moment, I stand in utter astonishment, my wide eyes locked onto his motionless form. It's almost surreal, the realization that I've resorted to such violence. But the urgency of the situation quickly sinks in, snapping me back to reality. Time is of the essence, and I must act swiftly. I go to his desk and into his drawer to grab his keycard and keys. A nice blue jacket lays on the bookcase, so I grab it, slip it on, and then search his desk for a pen. I coil my hair in a nice but messy bun, then promptly race to the door, open it, and steadily walk down the hall toward the double doors to exit. I keep a good pace because I don't want them to suspect anything. Reaching the elevator, I swipe the keycard.

Anxiety eats at me.

Hopefully, no one is on the elevator. Turning to look around, it seems like each camera is watching me. The doors open to emptiness. Without delay, I step on the elevator and press the first floor. My sweaty palms refuse to go away. The elevator moves down to the second floor, and the doors stay closed. Then, I approach the first. A camera looks down at me, and I keep my gaze forward. There is a guard station on the first floor with multiple guards, and hopefully, they'll not look my way. The doors open, and I contemplate going back up, but I've already hit the doctor, so I must keep going. I step off and don't look toward the guard station. I begin walking to the side exit Dr. Mocker previously took me through.

"Excuse me, madam?" I hear a voice.

My power walk turns into a full-force run. As fast as I can, I make my way to the door, swipe the keycard, pushing through the door without looking back.

ESCAPING

Soft, wet raindrops caress my face while the wind hums a lullaby in my ears. Coldness drapes over my body. I tell myself that it's not over yet. My shoes scrape against the hard cement pavement as I run through the courtyard.

"A white Range Rover," I whisper. The air from the words disperses into the atmosphere. I remember the doctor's car from when it was parked at my house, and he chased me in it. I run past the café windows, the fear in my heart thumping in my chest. "Stop," swims in the air to my ears. I turn for a mere second to see a short, chubby security guard chasing me. "Stop," rolls in again.

I envision the electrons powering my body, the mitochondria creating energy. "It's possible. I can do this," I whisper to myself as I continue to run, blocking out the "Stop" that plays in my head. Heat disperses from my inner soul, oiling my joints, fueling my muscles, expanding my lungs, and strengthening my heart as I run with every molecule in my body. Turning a corner, I see the car lot a short distance away.

"Hey," I hear someone yell. I turn and look. A tall, skinny man in white scrubs quickly approaches me. I hit the clicker on Dr. Mocker's car keys.

Beep, beep. It must be near.

"Stop!" comes from behind, loud and clear.

My left leg cramps up. "Come on, come on." I will myself to keep my pace as I enter the parking lot. The white Range Rover sticks out and catches my eye. "Thank you, Jesus!" I whisper, clicking "unlock" on the clicker. I run full force, ignoring the pain cruising down my leg. I open the door, jump in the car, and turn the ignition.

"It's not going to start," I speak aloud, but the engine roars to life. Relief washes over me once again. I put the gear in reverse and hit the gas, but the vehicle doesn't move. A grinding noise comes from the front of the truck. I knew something was going to go wrong!

The orderly reaches the truck and begins pulling on the door handle. I quickly lock the doors. "Open this door now," he yells as he bangs on the window. My foot presses down on the gas until the pedal touches the floor. White smoke comes out the back of the truck, the smell of rubber soaring in the air, but it still doesn't move. Glancing around, I look for a weapon or anything I can use in case I have to get out. Like lightning, a thought hits me.

The emergency brakes are on!

I push the brake, hoping it will come up, but it doesn't. More orderlies approach. Feeling under the collar of the steering wheel, I can't find the lever. Gently breathing in and out in an attempt to calm my mind, I close my eyes, reopen them, and the level jumps out at me. I pull it, hear the clicking sound, put the car back in reverse, and burn rubber out of the parking space.

Putting the car in drive, I witness one of the orderlies crumple to the ground. My foot slams on the accelerator once more, catapulting the vehicle out of the parking lot with reckless abandon. The car careens into the curb, sending it airborne for a moment and toppling a hapless trash can in its wake.

As the parking lot transforms into a winding driveway, a stark, white rectangular sign thrusts from the grass, sternly proclaiming a speed limit of 15 miles per hour. My foot remains unyielding, the speedometer needle hurtling past 45, the engine's roar echoing my urgency.

Suddenly, the trunk bounces ruthlessly over an unexpected speed bump, jolting the vehicle's front end skyward before crashing back to Earth. My grip on the steering wheel tightens, and I ease off the gas pedal momentarily, only to slam it back down with renewed determination.

A colossal, imposing black metal gate looms in the distant horizon alongside a rustic wooden-framed guardhouse. Without hesitation, I unleash the full might of the engine, hurtling toward the gate. A portly figure emerges from the guardhouse, stumbling with frantic urgency, and takes up a position directly in front of the gate. His wild, arm-waving gestures resemble a scorned lover, but I have no intention of slowing down. *Decisions, decisions.*

Do I hit him?

I can't.

Ripping my foot from the gas pedal, I slam my foot onto the brake with brutal force, my body catapulting forward. Panic clenches my chest as the realization hits that I won't halt in time. My frantic attempts to swerve right only result in a perilous overcorrection.

The world becomes a chaotic blur of twisted metal and splintering wood as I collide with the imposing gate, an agonizing crunch of metal on metal. Then, an unrelenting encounter with a towering oak tree, the sheer brutality of the impact, yanking me violently from my seat. My skull smashes into the windshield, and a searing, excruciating pain lances through my head. Excruciating pain surges through my body as I succumb to the inevitable darkness. My eyelids slam shut.

Footsteps wake me from a daze. Looking around, I see glass and blood. My head pounds, my ears ring, and pain surges through my limbs. A few minutes pass before everything that has just occurred is puzzled together. The SUV leans to the side, with its front slanted into a ditch. The overweight security guard stands next to the door of the vehicle. He holds a walkie-talkie in his hand up to his mouth. If I jump out, I'm sure I can outrun him and get past the gate, but then I would be on foot and easy to find. I reach up and adjust the rearview mirror. Behind me, I can see guards approaching on a golf cart.

Checking all over the SUV, I search for a weapon and find nothing but an empty energy drink can and some peppermint-flavored gum. Few options left, so I decide to run for it. Unlocking the door, I jump out and take off, running toward the gate. It must have caught the security guard off guard because it took him a few seconds to chase after me, but his speed wasn't fast. The golf cart sounds move into my hearing and let me know I have to hurry up and climb over. As I grip the hard, cool bars, I put my foot in a metal hole and start climbing. Pain radiates through my head, back, and neck, but I fight through it and keep moving. The brakes shirk on the golf cart as it comes to a stop. Moving as fast as I can, I refuse to look back; it will only slow me down.

"Get back down here," a raspy voice comes from the ground.

A sharp piece of metal sticks out and scrapes the side of my calf as I raise my foot and put it in another metal hole. Horrific pain cruises up and down near the scrape, and warm blood oozes out, but I try to put all my focus into getting over the gate.

"Summer, let's talk about this," the sound of Dr. Mocker's voice comes from below.

"Tell them what you did?" I scream back while gripping the metal spike and trying to use my strength to help pull me up.

"Go get her, please," I hear Dr. Mocker tell one of the guards.

Glancing down, I see a gym junkie swiftly moving toward the gate. Tightly holding the spikes, I put one leg over the gate, and the other leg follows. Now that I'm on the other side, I release the gate, jump to the asphalt, and land hard on my hurt leg. A few seconds pass while I sit there, consumed with pain. Adrenaline kicks back in, and I jump up, thinking I'm going to run, but instead, I limp as fast as I can toward a wooded area.

Maybe I can hide if I'm off the street.

My shoes crunch down on the tall, green grass, and the rest of my body hits the ground within seconds. The air runs out of my body, leaving me struggling to catch my breath. I'm face-down on the cold, damp grass, with moisture seeping through my clothing, touching my flesh. The security guard had tackled me to the ground. His hard chest mashes into my back.

"Stop moving. I don't want to hurt you," he says in a deep, hoarse voice. His breath smells like menthol and smoke. At this point, I know I've been conquered, and my only hope is that Ms. Charlie talks to her cousin and they are able to investigate Dr. Mocker.

A set of brown leather men's dress shoes approach. The security guard raises up a little and pulls my arms back, cuffing my wrist. He then gets up and helps me to my feet. My eyes move up from the brown shoes to khaki pants, then to a blood-stained white button-up shirt, and lastly. Dr. Mocker's face. A vertical gash runs down the front of his face, moving from his hairline right above his left eye. He walks toward me and, without saying a word, punctures my arm with a needle. Two more security guards approach.

"Everything is under control," Dr. Mocker tells the guards, then he points to the golf cart and instructs the guard holding my arm to walk me over and sit me down. My eyelids become heavy, and although I'm here, sitting on the cart next to the doctor and a guard, my mind wanders to the beautiful pine trees swaying in the wind, their small trunks indicating their youth, the birds gracefully gliding, chirping a symphony of peaceful sounds, the light blue lethargic clouds harmoniously dancing in the sky. The golf cart hits a speed hump, and it jolts me back to reality, and then the wheels rolling on the smooth asphalt soothes me back to a dreamy state.

Dr. Mocker's lips delicately press against my ear. "You can't get away from me," he whispers so gently. His warm, moisture-filled breath circles my ear canal. The sandalwood smell of his cologne mixes with the scent of brandy and fills the air. My head falls to his shoulder, and sleep embraces me.

SOMEONE HELP

If only I could awake somewhere else, somewhere pleasant. Maybe on a beach, lying in the sand, or on a hot summer's day. Not in this cold room with restraints on my arms and legs. The sleepy state I once was in has all the way escaped my body. My heart pounds hard and strong.

I was so close to escaping this place. I should have just hit the security guard and rammed the gate at full speed, but I'm not a killer. My stomach growls in the quietness, and although I haven't eaten since yesterday, my appetite is still surpassed by the urge to get out of this place and reveal the real Dr. Mocker to everyone.

"Help! Can someone come here, please?" I yell at the top of my lungs. My adrenaline surges with fuel to escape.

Pulling at the restraints, twisting, and trying to turn, I'm unable to get loose.

Maria walks into the room.

"You're finally awake."

"Please take these restraints off."

"I can't. You hit the doctor over the head with a bottle and tried to leave. What were you thinking?"

"Dr. Mocker is a killer. He killed my husband and his wife," I scream.

"Calm down."

"Did you hear what I just said?"

"Yes, I heard you. The doctor already told us you would say that."

"It's the truth," I yell.

"You're scheduled for ECT in an hour, so just try to relax. I'm going to alert the doctor that you have woken up."

"Wait," I shout to Maria, but my words land on deaf ears. She walks out the door, and I hear her footsteps continuing down the hall. Tugging and yanking, I try my hardest to get loose, but all of my efforts go to waste. It seems as if there is nothing left for me to do but lay here until they take the restraints off.

Dr. Mocker enters the room. A bandage sits on his head over the spot where the gash sits. He's dressed in white scrubs instead of his usual khakis and button-up.

"How's your head?" I ask him.

He looks at me and smirks, then grabs the chair that sits by the desk and puts it next to the bed. He sits down, crosses his legs, and looks at me, smiling.

"How do the restraints feel?"

My eyes roll.

"I figured I would give you a quick consultation before our ECT session."

"You're really enjoying this," I say to him.

"You have no idea," he says, rubbing his hand along my arm.

"You don't have to do this. Just let me go, please."

"So you can run away and tell everyone?"

Dr. Mocker stands above me and rubs his hand along my breast.

"Stop, please," I beg him.

"Who's going to stop me?" he asks with a smile.

The door of the room begins creaking, and Dr. Mocker quickly takes his hand from my breast and drops it to his side. Maria walks in.

"She hasn't eaten yet. Should I get her something from the cafeteria?"

"Great idea, Maria," he tells her, and Maria turns and walks back out of the room.

"Wait, Maria! Wait!" I scream, but she doesn't return.

"This is my hospital. You're in my territory, and you're either going to get on board, or I'll torture you, then eventually kill you, and guess what? It will look like an accident; no one will question it. No one cares about you, Summer. Not one person has come up here since you have been in here. You have no one."

"I thought you weren't a killer?"

"If it comes down to me or you, it's going to be you. Trust me."

Closing my eyes, I squeeze my eyelids together, trying to keep tears from coming down.

Dr. Mocker walks over to my nightstand, grabs the notebook he gave me, and walks over to the door.

"See you in a little bit," he tells me and walks out. A little relief flows through my body as he exits the room. The sound of footsteps bustling in from under the doorway gives life to the quiet room. The air from the air conditioner whistles in and floods my body with coldness. Glancing around, I spot the sheet and covers below my feet at the foot of the bed. They could have at least covered me up.

"I'm back," Maria says as she enters the room.

I raise my head to look over at her and drop it back onto the pillow.

"Are you going to undo my hands?" I ask her.

"I'll undo one."

Maria sits my tray on the desk and begins unfastening my left arm.

"Maria, did you know Dr. Mocker and Delisa are having an affair?"

She ignores my comments.

"When I first got here, why did you tell me Dr. Mocker likes the ladies?"

"I never told you that. Okay, your arm is undone. I'm going to sit here while you eat," Maria tells me as she places the tray on my lap.

"Dr. Mocker is not who you think he is," I tell her.

"Please, stop with this."

I look down at the tray. It consists of broth and water.

"Is this my food?"

"You can't have anything heavy before the ECT."

"Can you undo the other arm and my legs so I can go to the bathroom?"

"I can bring you a bedpan," she tells me.

"Okay, thank you."

Maria walks out of the room, and I wait a few seconds before beginning to hastily undo my other arm. Once it's undone, I reach down and undo my legs, jump out of bed, and quickly grab my tray, wasting the broth onto the floor. I run to the side of the door and stand there, tray held high in the air, waiting for Maria to re-enter.

My adrenaline is in full force. I feel there's nothing I can't do. Maria walks through the door and stops before the door closes.

I take a step toward her and hit her head with my tray as hard as I could. Without a moment's hesitation, I seize the bedpan and yank the keycard hanging from her shirt, my fingers trembling with urgency. The corridor echoes with the ominous approach of footsteps, an unsettling rhythm that propelled me into a frantic sprint.

Closing the distance to the double security doors and the elevator, my pulse races, sweat beading on my forehead. With adrenaline-fueled agility, I swipe the keycard through the reader, the electronic lock relenting with a soft beep. The elevator doors obediently slide open, revealing a refuge from the impending chaos.

Inside the confined space, I swipe the keycard once more and, with trembling fingers, press the illuminated "1" button. The doors begin their inexorable journey to closure, a chilling symphony of ticking seconds. A uniformed guard, desperation etched on his face, sprints toward me, his outstretched hand mere inches from the retreating doors.

A triumphant grin creeps across my face as the elevator doors seal shut with a final, unforgiving inch, leaving the guard futilely pounding against the metal barrier. They'll probably be waiting for me on the first floor. I push the "2." Maybe I can get off there and find the stairs, or at least somewhere I can hide until I figure out what to do next. The doors slowly open, and two guards stand before me. Swinging the bedpan as hard as possible, I aim for their heads. One of the guards sticks out a device. It comes toward me; before I know it, electrical volts surge up and down my body. I fall to the ground, shaking. They stand over me, watching, laughing, and conversing as if this is normal. When I stop shaking, one of the guards pulls me out of the elevator, and the other one picks up his walkie-talkie and puts it to his mouth.

"Bring a wheelchair?"

It's not apparent to me whether seconds are passing or minutes, but the pain radiates throughout my body. Today has been a day of absolute torment. Spectators gather, watching me lay on the hard floor. The elevator opens, and Dr. Mocker and a nurse stand near me with a hospital bed.

"Load her onto the bed, and let's take her for her ECT session," says Dr. Mocker.

"She's just been tasered. Shouldn't we wait? Wouldn't it have an effect on her?"

"No! She needs it now," Dr. Mocker tells one of the nurses. His face now swollen.

The guards lift me onto the bed, and Dr. Mocker takes a needle from his front scrub pocket. He pops the top off and sticks me in my arm. They then begin rolling me down the hall. A smile covers the doctor's face.

"How did you know what floor to come to?" he whispers so only I can hear him.

My eyes meet the bright lights hanging above, and I watch them as they push me until my eyes finally close.

Awaking in a cold room, my head pounds and my body shivers from the cold air blowing down on my body. Glancing around the room, I have no idea where I am or how I got here. The room resembles a hospital room without all the extra equipment hospitals have. My body aches, and sharp pains run down my leg. Attempting to get out of bed, my body feels limp and drained of energy. I slowly walk over to the door and try to open it, but it's locked. Balling my fist, I raise it and pound on the door. The door clicks, and I turn the handle to find it opens to a hallway. I slowly walk down the narrow hallway and approach a nurse's station.

"Where am I?" I ask a lady dressed in white scrubs.

"I'm sorry, Summer, but the doctor has to talk to you, and he will explain everything to you. He's not here now but will return tomorrow morning."

"Can you at least tell me where I am?"

"You're at Brunswick Mental Institute. You had an ECT done earlier, and you should lay down and get some rest."

"Mental Institute? What is ECT?"

"The doctor will explain everything to you in the morning. Let me walk you to your room."

The nurse comes from around the station, and we return to the room. I sit on the bed and stare at the wall, wondering what's going on with my mind because I do not know why I am here. Footsteps sound off outside my room. Looking toward the door, I see a folded piece of paper glide along the floor to the foot of my bed. I walk over, pick it up, and unfold it. A strong feeling makes me feel as if it's my handwriting, and it reads:

Dr. Mocker killed your husband and his wife because they were having an affair. Don't trust anyone except Whitney and Ms. Charlie. Ms. Charlie is supposed to notify the police about what Dr. Mocker did.

Dear Reader,

Thank you so much for taking the time to read my book. I hope you enjoyed it as much as I enjoyed writing it. Your support means the world to me and helps me continue to share stories with readers like you.

If you found this book engaging, thought provoking, or simply enjoyable, I would greatly appreciate it if you could take a moment to leave a review on Amazon. Your feedback not only helps me improve but also assists other readers in discovering new favorites.

Leaving a review is simple and doesn't take much time, but it makes a huge difference. Whether it's a few sentences or a full review, your insights are invaluable.

Thank you once again for your support and for being a part of this journey.

Warm regards,
Ingrid Jennings